Roberta Samuels

MISSING

A Modern Art Masterpiece in a French Medieval Village

ART MYSTERY NOVELLA SERIES

Red Penguin BOOKS

CONTENTS

PROLOGUE

1944, TOULOUSE, FRANCE

Sonia ducked into the café right across the street from the main train station in Toulouse, *la Gare Matabiau*. She flicked the rain from her coat. It was one of her own designs, still stylish although well-worn after all these years of hard use. Her eyes adjusted to the gloomy interior and its haze of cigarette smoke. Behind her, gruff cries of "Halt. Papieren!" continued as Nazi soldiers conducted their street check of the area bordering the Canal du Midi. She'd been lucky it had started several yards ahead of her, allowing her a moment to slip into the closest shelter she could find, the modest and workaday Café de la Gare.

She made her way across the tiled floor to the old-fashioned zinc-top bar. Outside the thunder rumbled and rain pitter-pattered on the windowpanes. It felt a little safer standing there with the assorted other patrons. A little warmer too, out of the wind.

Toulouse was known for the hot sun which usually baked its stunning rose-brick architecture. Today's blustery weather was the exception that proved the rule.

At Sonia's request, the bartender reached for the house red, his gaze levelled over her shoulder to the street. Pedestrians lined up in the drizzle, huddling over the identity papers they offered up to equally sodden, foul-tempered soldiers.

She sipped at her glass of wine, keeping a wary eye on the street. It was 1944 and the Nazi takeover of France had become progressively more draconian since 1940. The subjugated French population had learned at their peril to be fearful of Nazi roundups and reprisals.

"Merde," the bartender mumbled as he moved away and made himself busy.

Sonia stiffened but refused to turn around as the Nazi soldiers entered the cafe and bellowed, "Papieren!" She watched in the mirror behind the bar as they grabbed the proffered IDs from a handful of customers. They were SS, the most feared. She saw the death head symbol on their caps.

Had they been tipped off or was this a random shake-down? *L'occupant,* as some Frenchmen called the Nazi invaders used these *rafles* to uncover stray Jews, gypsies, members of the Resistance and other undesirables. In this case, the soldiers seemed to be following up a lead or a denouncement.

With a sense of dread, Sonia turned back against the bar and slowly withdrew the identity card she was required to always carry from her purse. The feeling was a familiar one— one that grew in strength each time she performed this ritual. She had barely managed to escape a spot check like this on the train from Montpellier earlier that day.

Her hand was steady as she readied her card, her gaze drifting to where the customs stamp almost obscured her place of origin in the Russian Empire's Pale of Settlement, now Ukraine, where Jews were sometimes allowed to reside. Now forty-nine years old, she had been living in France for more than thirty years and had established herself as one of the most important avant-garde artists of the time. She and her husband Robert Delaunay were among the first artists to desert representational art and master abstraction.

She felt completely French. In a fortuitous twist, her married name—DELAUNAY—had been stamped in big letters across the top of her identity card, covering her birth name, Sarah Stern. So, a cursory glance could miss this information, but an eagle eye...

The SS stormtroopers were nearer now. So close she could smell the damp off the shoulders of their uniforms. One of the men was in a foul mood, snatching and snapping, and surely too young for his station. Her stomach cramped and she fought to maintain her poise. A quick glance upward and she caught his cold, blue eyes. *Mistake.* Hurriedly she swung her gaze away. It fell on a slim, grey-haired man, sitting hunched at a table in the corner over his espresso cup.

He winked.

Her face would have lit up with surprise and pleasure if she hadn't been so desperately composed. *Willy!*

The soldiers were two patrons away when they were summoned curtly to the door by their superior officer, a hard-bitten older man clad in a leather trench-coat. Obeying the command, the young soldiers tossed the papers of the patron they were inspecting to the floor and turned on their heels.

There was a scuffle outside in the street as some unlucky

pedestrian, dishevelled and ashen faced, was manhandled into a German armored van which had drawn up by the cafe terrace. The soldiers all piled in after him and departed for headquarters.

"Another?" The bartender was back by her elbow, bottle poised. "You look like you need it."

"Please," Sonia answered distractedly. She paid for the wine, took her glass and moved through the tables toward the far corner and Willy, her ex-husband. He'd always been a kind man, and Sonia felt enormous affection for him. She had met him when she was first starting out as a young artist in Paris. Willy, Wilhelm Uhde, an art critic and collector, was the owner of prominent art galleries in Paris, where he exhibited her work along with Pablo Picasso. He was eleven years her senior, but his marriage proposal had lifted her into a new world. One where she could flourish. And yes, she had been a shield for his promiscuity with men but, in return, he had granted her the freedom to live in the French capital and paint under the shelter of their marriage of convenience.

Sonia smiled as he rose to greet her with a kiss on each cheek. It was impossible that he was here in this cafe. They hadn't seen each other since before the war. So much time, so many losses, and now, simply the joy of meeting up with an old friend. Tears pricked her eyes. "Oh, Willy." She reached for his hand.

His fingers tightened around her own. "I can't believe it's you."

"Me neither." She sank into the seat opposite.

"I admit that I was panicking," he said, his eyes wide and vaguely haunted. "For you, I mean. I was quaking in my boots, what with your papers and everything."

Willy was alluding to her Jewish heritage. Sonia's married

name, Delaunay, was alright, but her given name was Sarah Stern and that, combined with her place of birth, would mark her as a Jewess, something she had never really thought about until the Nazis came along. "Where's Robert?" he suddenly asked, noting someone was missing, namely her husband.

"Oh, Willy." Her face softened. "Robert died on the operating table in Montpellier at the clinic there. Cancer."

"Ah, chérie." His grip on her fingers tightened. "Such a loss. For you. For art. For all of us."

"We're surrounded by loss," she said. "War is loss. Totally and utterly. The doctors did everything they could to save him, but it was too late." The weight of the past years felt heavier now she had a friend to share it with.

"You and Robert were the aristocracy of Montmartre." Willy grew misty eyed, "the king and queen of form and color. Oh, those days..." He trailed off with a sigh. Lost in memories, his face softened. "What on earth are you doing here?" he asked. "You should have stayed on *la Côté d'Azur* where I heard you were hiding."

"Things got too dangerous there," she said. She explained that she had been living with Dadaist artists Jean and Sophie Arp before they made it into neutral Switzerland with their Swiss papers. "I had to leave, too, but I have no Swiss passport. So, I decided to come to Toulouse knowing that from here I could make my way to Tarbes or St Gaudens. From these border towns, some people are smuggled over the Pyrenees into Spain where Robert and I lived in the last war."

Sonia and Robert Delaunay had been safe in Spain during the First World War. Sonia had started a ceramics business in Madrid and had found work there designing costumes for the Diaghilev Ballet Company and the famous *Ballets Russes*.

Willy gave her a look of pure pity. *She was grasping at*

straws. "What are you going to do, Sonia? Have you arranged anywhere to go?"

She shrugged and drained her glass. "Not really."

Rising to his feet, Willy grabbed his raincoat, then offered her his hand. "Come with me."

"Where?"

He didn't answer until they were out on the street. "Do you remember Tzara?"

"Tristan Tzara? The poet?"

Tristan was an old friend. A dear friend. Someone she'd known from her old life, her pre-war life, her artist's life in Paris before it was so brutally stripped away. Sonia had designed costumes for his avant-garde play, and Tzara had written poetic phrases to be woven into her *simultané* fashions.

Willy nodded, pulled up his collar and led her towards the bike stand across the street.

"I know where he is," he said. "And Paul and Céline, too. They've made it all the way from Belgium."

Sonia looked at him astonished.

"You'd be surprised how many we have, Sonia. And you must come, too."

"Come where?" She was reeling. *Dadaist poet Paul Dermée and his wife, Céline Arnaud, the art critic?*

"They're at the chateau, too. We have a sort of commune," Willy explained. "It's a big rambling place in the medieval French village of Grisolles. Our friend, Jean Cassou, who is also living there, unearthed it and rented it for us. We all live there quietly and gently and draw no more attention than need be. At least until this war is over. You'll be safe there, Sonia. Please, you must come."

She watched as Willy attempted to pull a bicycle from the

many stacked haphazardly against the railings of the Gare Matabiau train station.

"Let me," she smiled, impressing him with the ease with which she disentangled the front wheel from the other bike's pedal. "Hop on," she exclaimed. "I can sit on the back wheel rack."

Soon they were wobbling across Rue Bayard and out onto Boulevard du Bon Repos.

"It'll take about an hour to get to the village," Willy shouted over the wind tousling her short brown curls. "I can't wait for you to see our hideaway and meet up with everybody again."

It was unimaginable the turn of fate, Sonia mused. Thank heavens for the spot check that had sent her into the Café de la Gare.

Wasn't life sometimes just like that? One action could lead to a delight or a debacle, safety or insecurity...

———

From the viewpoint of my summer house about 50 miles north from Toulouse and my vantage point eighty years later, I, Barbara Waldheim, identified with Sonia Delaunay. Certainly, there were more differences in our situations than similarities. Sonia had lived a long time ago in another era, a time replete with danger, especially for a Russian Jew and an artist with no sympathy for the Vichy government. I was safe and secure. No one was threatening me. I was an amateur painter, not a famous artist. I was an American whose forebears had come to the United States from the same Eastern European shtetl area which Sonia had left to go to Paris in 1910. My ancestors were poor. Her Saint Petersburg relatives were wealthy. Yet, I too, made snap decisions and trusted the universe to pull my irons out of the fire.

At the present time in 2014, I was dealing with the consequences of a hasty decision to buy an old house in a small French medieval village. Little did I suspect that Sonia Delaunay, an artist I admired, would have a close connection with my little town. Nor that I, one small action leading to another, would get involved in a Sonia Delaunay mystery story.

CHAPTER ONE

A LEAKY ROOF

2014, MONTPEZAT DE QUERCY, NEAR TOULOUSE, FRANCE

It must be an illusion.

I was standing in the dining room of the 15th century townhouse in the heart of the exquisite, medieval French village of Montpezat de Quercy, which I had just purchased. It was a stormy spring day, and I was admiring the little courtyard out the French doors when I thought I heard water dripping.

No, it can't be, I told myself. *It's just the sound of the rain pattering on the garden furniture.*

The sound seemed to be coming from behind me. Curious, I traced the dripping noise to a strange, recessed alcove by the front door. These medieval houses were full of quirky spaces whose original purpose was obscure to a 21st century owner like me, and a new owner at that.

Merde! Bordel de merde! When I turned on the light, I saw small rivulets of water inching down the wall and making little *plinks* when they landed on the tile floor.

I touched the wall to double check. *Oh my God! It was water alright!* The plaster was wet, not damp, but wet.

Saturated, in fact! Little beads of rainwater were trickling down from the floor above.

I was outraged. *It couldn't be true!* What about the vaunted new roof the seller assured me was constructed from a completely waterproof high-tech material. As it hardly ever rained in the Tarn-et-Garonne region, I'd taken his word as a gentleman. Only weather like this could have proved otherwise.

I focused my attention on the funny depression in the floor where water was pooling. I liked the tile there, which was newer than the rest of the floor. It was a 19th century addition in a blue-green and orange checkerboard pattern. Old-fashioned but very pretty. Did it seem to be attracting the water? Or was I dreaming?

Oh, how I wished Sam were here with me to help deal with this catastrophe instead of back in Florida accumulating vacation time at his hydraulics valve company. I had preceded him to Montpezat to get the house ready for our first summer together in our new place.

The previous fall, we had bought this medieval townhouse in a beautiful village in the south of France, near Toulouse. A selling point had been the charming renovations. The house had been modernized by the previous owner and had a brand-new roof but still retained most of its original features and 15th century cachet. Now it had water pooling on the floor, and I felt like crying.

In a fever of activity, I went up to the attic, tracked down the source of the leaks and put down buckets and tarps to catch the water. Luckily, the thunderstorm abated as I sat among the dust and cobwebs and considered my options. I was disheartened but equally determined to seek redress. This situation was unfair to me, the new and proud owner of a charming, if very old, property in an equally very old village.

Let me introduce myself. I am Barbara Waldheim, an American, a divorcée and Francophile who speaks decent French after careers as a French teacher and French tour escort. I moved to France alone after my divorce two years earlier and bought a fixer-upper in a neighboring village, determined to make a fresh start and have adventures *à la française*, among them a steamy romance with a Frenchman. I was on my own, my children were grown, and I had enough money to retire on, so why not try something new. After my divorce, I needed to reestablish my independence, to learn to stand on my own two feet and take responsibility for my actions.

I bought an impressive property located on the edge of an award-winning flowering village twelve kilometers away from Montpezat de Quercy, the village where I was now. My former house was called Pech Menal. It was built in the 18th century and was in the hamlet of Cayrièch on several acres of land where cows, the big, white Aquitaines native to the region, grazed picturesquely. The exteriors and the mechanical systems of the farmhouse, barn, and stable had been beautifully renovated by a French nobleman who then left them half-baked, waiting for the finishing touches—a real kitchen and bathroom, an indoor toilet, tile floors, a wood stove, landscaping—which would make them liveable and loveable.

Advised by my real estate agent, who loved the place, and my helpful neighbors across the dirt track, I took on this challenge and lavished time and money making Pech Menal a showplace. I spent two long years bringing the project to a successful conclusion—boosting my self-confidence and decision-making skills in the bargain.

I accomplished my goals. I completed the renovations, and I met and dallied with many alluring Frenchmen, proving to myself that I was still desirable. Everything was going according to plan when the apple cart was overturned by a delightful but unexpected development—to my surprise, I fell in love with a fellow American and not a handsome Frenchman, as I long fantasized.

I met Sam Spitz, my new love, the past winter while I was back in Florida, my main residence. Sam was born in Romania, and he had emigrated to the United States via Canada from Israel in the 1970s.

On the face of it, a rather spoiled dilettante like me and a rough-hewn, less-affluent man like Sam might not seem that well suited. In fact, our mutual attraction and esteem for one another ran deep and strong.

Like me, Sam loved the work I had done on the old farmhouse, but the big property was difficult and expensive to maintain. More importantly, Sam was not ready to retire so although he could vacation with me in France in the summers, for the foreseeable future we would spend the winters in Florida, another reason that my new partner and I didn't need or want such a fancy property as Pech Menal. We wanted to be free to travel and not be tied down by too many household responsibilities.

As impressive as Pech Menal was, we realized we preferred to be in the center of a bustling village with its cafés, restaurants, and shops, animated by a variety of townspeople we might befriend or who might befriend us. And so, I sold Pech Menal and Sam and I moved 20 minutes away to the fruit tree-covered hills of Montpezat de Quercy.

Our new village of 1,500 souls was one of the most charming in the region. Montpezat's picture-perfect town square with its charming limestone arcades and half-timbered houses untouched since the Middle Ages made it exceptionally lovely. Our new house was just off the square in this story-book setting.

The icing on the cake of this gorgeous town was la collégiale de Saint Martin, the magnificent church just down the hill. From our bedroom window, we had an eye-popping view of its distinctive 14th century bell tower and out to the rolling hills and Pyrenees Mountains beyond. The sole church in the village, Saint Martin's was still active for Sunday and holiday worship and many weddings and funeral services were solemnized there.

As imposing and historic as Saint Martin's was, it was inside the church where the real treasure was to be found. The collégiale contained a set of 16th century tapestries woven in Flanders commissioned to hang tailor-made in its apse where they had been on display for five hundred years, except for wartime. In time of danger, they had been hidden for safekeeping, probably buried.

The stained-glass windows of the church were not exceptional, although there was a nice rose window above the entry door. The window in the first chapel as you entered had been damaged during a modern war and had been replaced with a window of clear glass and ironwork in a simple pattern called *grisaille*. That seemed regrettable, but you had to expect losses and damage to such an old building.

In a former time, this broken window would have been replaced by a copy of the old one. However, such modern recreations were no longer thought acceptable. The new trend in restoring monuments and artwork required that any repair or substitution should be apparent and not try to disguise itself by fading in.

My new little village, like much of the surrounding area, had suffered harsh treatment during WWII when it was occupied by the brutal 2nd SS Division Das Reich. To commemorate the end of the war, many streets in town had been renamed. The name of our street was La Rue de la Liberation, changed from Windy Street at the war's end. The town square was renamed Place de la Résistance and not far away was La Rue du 8 Mai 1945, named for the exact date of VE Day, Victory in Europe Day.

Best of all, Montpezat was a real town, not just a tourist attraction. There was a butcher, a baker, a florist, two hairdressers and two garage mechanics. The grocery store was small but well-stocked in case you missed market day on Saturday. Just outside of the central village core was a public swimming pool, soccer field, and campground.

Our new house looks old because it is old, 15th century. The seller, Monsieur Hernandez, assured us the electricity and plumbing have all been redone and the roof is new—but as I sit catching the rain in my buckets, I am questioning the veracity of his promises. Sam wouldn't be arriving for two weeks, so I was on my own for the time being.

What to do? I mustn't let myself be taken advantage of. The seller shouldn't have put one over on me.

As I sat watching the drips slow down to a halt, an idea occurred to me. When Sam and I bought the place from Monsieur Hernandez, we also purchased some pieces of furniture, like a Moroccan chest and a giant desk, which we kind of had to buy since it will never fit back down the staircase. I could never figure out how the owner had gotten it up in the first place! In addition, we also bought the antique tapestry hanging in the front hall and a set of modern bar stools in the kitchen, along with some very fancy French beds. I hadn't yet paid for these items. Perhaps they could be a bargaining chip in my negotiation with Monsieur Hernandez over the roof repairs.

I decided to consult my Parisian friend, Micheline Dubosc, about this idea. Micheline was a font of knowledge and might have some hard-headed advice for me. I gave her a call after dinner.

"Barbara," Micheline said, her authoritative voice held an air of sympathy that heartened me over the phone. "*Écoute*, anyone can make a mistake. Your decision to purchase the property was made rather hastily. I suspected that you might have problems when you showed me the old townhouse last year. I told you to be careful. Maybe, put the house back on the market, *n'est-ce pas?* Why not list it in *Particulier à Particulier*."

"What's *Particulier à Particulier*, Micheline?"

Micheline didn't waste time scolding me. She was trying to help. That's what I loved about her.

"It's a classified ad news sheet where private parties can buy and sell directly among each other, everything from houses to cars to lawn mowers to furniture."

"But Micheline, I don't want to resell," I whined. "I just bought this house. I love it and the village, too. I want to complain to the seller. Monsieur Hernandez assured me the roof was brand new. He told me they had put a special high-tech material under the roof tiles which was absolutely *étanche*, waterproof."

"In that case, send him a *lettre recommandée avec accusé de réception*, explaining the problem."

"What's a *lettre recommandée*?" I asked.

"Go to the post office and they will give you the form.

Monsieur Hernandez is obliged to notify you that he received your letter, and he has a week to reply."

"*D'accord,* Micheline. Thanks. I'll send him a *lettre recommandée* tomorrow."

As was often the case after a chat with Micheline, I hung up the phone feeling much better.

————

In the days immediately following, I exchanged *lettres recommandées* with Monsieur Hernandez as Micheline advised. I threatened to withhold payment for the furniture until he fixed the roof.

His reply more or less said that I didn't have a leg to stand on since I had bought the house *en état,* meaning an 'as is' condition. If I refused to pay him for the furniture, he would take legal action against me. Furthermore, he explained that he had never made any bones about the fact that his house renovations were more about *le look* than expert workmanship. I had run up against a wall. A water-stained wall. I had to face the fact that I had exchanged my former French house, Pech Menal, where everything had been restored to the highest standard, *aux normes,* for a charming hovel.

As Micheline pointed out, I had acted rashly. I should have had the house inspected. I shouldn't have taken the seller's word on faith. However, despite these problems, I was still under the spell of my cute new house and its modest purchase price. It had been my decision to move to Montpezat de Quercy, and I would make it work. This was my new mantra.

Undaunted by the seller's uncooperative response to my *lettre recomandée,* I had a new idea that involved the workman who had done such a poor job on my roof. Hernandez had left me his name on a receipt. I could contact him directly to complain about the leaks and see what he would do to rectify the problem.

I dialed the roofer's number, feeling full of hope and well-justified indignation. The voice that came on at the end of the line sounded quite young. A baby was wailing in the background. I explained who I was and my problem.

Straining to talk over the crying baby, the young man explained to me that although the geotextile he had used under the roof tiles was indeed impermeable, he was a novice at roofing. He had not yet learned how to make the edges of the roof as waterproof as the middle!

I exploded, "*Ce n'est pas possible! Vous n'avez pas honte?* Aren't you ashamed of yourself? You don't even know how to repair your own faulty handiwork?"

"That's more or less the situation. *C'est plus ou moins le cas,*" he replied, abashed, as the baby cried louder and louder in the background. "Monsieur Hernandez is my brother-in-law, and he hired me to help since we needed the money. My wife and I are moving out of the area."

Checkmate. I felt very foolish, but neither could I afford to redo the roof, at least not yet. For the time being, I'd just have to put my faith in the dry summer climate of the *Tarn-et-Garonne* and my system of tarpaulins, *des bâches,* and buckets, *des sceaux,* in the attic.

CHAPTER TWO

HIDING IN PLAIN SIGHT
THE ARTIST RESIDENTS OF THE CHATEAU DE GRISOLLES

Crunch. Squeal. Lurch.

That's the gears on my used Citroen Xsara station wagon. Or rather, me trying to make it to the airport in time for Sam's flight. He was returning for our summer break, and I was madly excited to see him after too long a separation.

Driving down the autoroute, I was making good time when I got a text message from Sam. *Oh no!* His plane was delayed by two hours taking off from Paris due to an air controller slow-down. Damn those *grèves!*

Grève is the word for strike in French. They happened a lot in the spring and summer when more people were traveling. Often it was the railroad workers, *les cheminots* of the SNCF striking for better benefits. Now it was the personnel at Charles de Gaulle airport.

In France, strikers did not necessarily give advance notice of the disruption they intended to cause. Tons of tomatoes or truckloads of milk might be dumped on a national highway in a spur of the moment expression of the farmers' discontent with their margins. The more confusion and upheaval they created, the better. Striking workers and work slow-downs were a normal part of life and were tolerated as a time-honored strategy of bringing the government's attention to an issue.

Now I had two hours to kill. I didn't want to just sit at the airport waiting for Sam. I was too wound up. I got off the highway at the neighboring town of Grisolles to fill up the gas tank. Grisolles had a few attractions, the Musee de Calbet and a chateau.

I'd already visited the museum, which featured the poetry and paintings of its namesake, Thomas Calbet, so I was thrilled when I spotted the banner stretched across the road announcing an art exhibition at the nearby Chateau de Grisolles, *Hiding in Plain Sight—The Artist Residents of the Chateau de Grisolles*. I followed the road a little way out of *centre ville* to the imposing gates of the castle. I parked the car in the grassy space provided, paid my entry fee at a little booth, and was admitted into the cobblestone courtyard.

The chateau was huge, consisting of several wings dating from different periods in French history. I was on my own; there seemed to be no other visitors that morning. I followed a sign which showed the way to the start of the exhibition.

In the palatial entry hall, the exhibit was introduced by a blowup group photo from 1944 in which all the artists sheltering at the chateau during World War II were identified by name. I only recognized one of them, the abstract painter, Sonia Delaunay. An amateur painter myself, I had always admired her use of color and her sense of design. Her work was so cheery, but not saccharine. It seemed deceptively simple and like all great art, it belied the expertise and planning which had gone into it.

The description below the photo indicated that Delaunay

and the four men and three women knew one another from the art scene in Paris before the war. One was Paris gallery owner Willy Uhde. Another was journalist Florent Fels. Jean Cassou, the head of the Musée d'Art Moderne in Paris before the war and also a poet, was flanked by Céline Arnaud and her husband Paul Dermée, two poets and art critics from Belgium. Germaine Krull, an anti-Vichy photographer, and surrealist poet Tristan Tzara were also among the octet.

On the opposite wall, there was another grainy photo showing the same group socializing during an apéritif hour on the terrace adjacent to the hall that I could see out the French doors. *Had they traveled together or ended up by chance at the chateau de Grisolles while fleeing the Nazis farther north?* From the Nazi viewpoint, they were all undesirable subversives.

Tzara and Céline Arnaud were originally Romanian. Many were Communists, and some were also Jews. Cassou had been arrested by the Germans for Resistance activities and escaped. All of them were proponents or creators of the 'decadent' art the Nazis wanted to eradicate.

It seemed the artists managed to keep up their creative activities—photographing, painting, writing poetry, and art criticism—because, luckily for them, Grisolles was in the Free French Zone sheltered from the worst abuses of the Vichy government, which was closely collaborating with the German occupiers up north. It was only at the end of the war that Vichy co-opted the southern half of the country and cracked down on its inhabitants.

I was hoping to see a Sonia Delaunay painting, but there didn't seem to be one, just some excerpts from her diary detailing her time in hiding at the chateau.

Next stop was the beautiful garden where the hiding artists had a big *potager*, vegetable garden, which supplied them with fresh produce. The refugees lived quietly, limiting their interactions with the surrounding farmers with whom they maintained good relations.

On the covered terrace where the group used to eat in fine weather, the table was laid for the eight refugees with place cards inscribed with their names marking each seat around the massive mahogany table. On the table itself were some placards with excerpts from Sonia's diary mentioning absent friends and describing the arty bohemian atmosphere of the prewar years she and the others had enjoyed in Paris. They had partied with Picasso, Braque, Jean Arp and his wife, artist Sophie Tauber, the Chagalls, Fernand Léger—a who's who of the art world of that time.

The exhibit continued onto the second floor. I checked my phone, and I still had time to spare. I followed the guiding arrow up the stairs in the Tudor wing to the bedroom that Sonia had occupied during her stay. The room had a lovely view out to the Garonne River. In this room, the entries from her diary on display were more personal. I could imagine her sitting at the little desk by the window writing them:

> *I almost have to pinch myself to believe this lucky turn of events. I am in a safe haven where I can recover from Robert's death and contemplate my future life on my own without him. I am deeply comforted by the condolences of this group who knew and appreciated Robert and knew well what a formidable couple we two artists had been.*

I felt her fear in the passages that spoke to the uncertainty of living through a war, especially hiding out as a Jewish refuge. She described the lights of the chateau going out unexpectedly and the muffled sounds of artillery and gunshots in the distance. German, Allied, or Resistance skirmishes? She didn't know for sure, but it was unsettling.

It must have been a very difficult time, indeed. Everything was up in the air. All the refugees sheltering at the chateau were in limbo—and in danger.

As instructed, I retraced my steps down the curving staircase and out a doorway to the chateau's private chapel where I saw a photo of a priest on the wall. The tag said he was Frère Raymond as an older man. He was standing at the altar smiling.

The exhibit explained how Frère Raymond in his younger years had become friendly with the former museum head Jean Cassou through their work together in the local Resistance movement. The postulant priest was ideally placed to gather information about German troop movements as he moved from parish to parish helping the presiding cleric in each district prepare the vestments and communion wafers for Sunday mass in the many little churches scattered around the region.

I was surprised to learn that Sonia and these other important figures of the *avant garde* movement had resided near my little village. Who would have suspected that these minor art world luminaries and the Resistance hero Jean Cassou had lived and worked here in Grisolles unmolested from 1943 to 1944. It didn't seem that the villagers actively shielded them. They just went about their business or looked the other way. The French were often known for their laissez-faire attitude toward people who were different.

Here I came upon an incredible part of the exhibit. It seemed that just before Liberation, Frère Raymond warned the artists that their cover was blown, and they were about to be detained. Since Sonia Delaunay had nowhere to go, Frère

Raymond offered to hide her at his parents' farm in Montpezat de Quercy. That's right, my very own adoptive village!

Luckily for them all, the war ended before they had to put that plan into effect, but Sonia had left a touching passage in her diary, expressing her eternal gratitude to the priest's parents in Montpezat. She vowed to repay them someday if she could find a way.

At the exit, I wrote a little note of appreciation in the guest book with my Florida address, got back in the car, and resumed my trip to the airport. The break had done me good by giving me something else to think about for a while.

I was just on time. I even had a few minutes to get a snack before Sam's plane landed. It was so exciting! We were going to have a great summer together in our new house.

CHAPTER THREE

SAM ARRIVES FOR THE SUMMER

"Babe!" Sam swept me up in a big kiss that garnered appreciative glances from passersby at Arrivals.

French people are tolerant of demonstrative displays of affection in public. I was flustered but happy. Sam always flustered me, and he enjoyed the effect he had on me.

We took a step back and took a moment to look at one another after our month apart. Sam looked fit and tanned as usual. He was medium height, lithe, and athletic in build. He had dark brown hair greying at the temples, which lent him a somewhat distinguished air when he wore his glasses. His most outstanding features were his dark brown eyes, which sparkled like agates, and his generous smile. There was a beauty mark on his upper lip and when he opened his mouth to speak, his distinctive gravelly voice had the trace of an accent or a cadence that was foreign.

The long flight did not seem to have tired him out at all. His clothes were pressed, and he was neatly dressed as always. Looking me over with appreciation, he gave me a saucy wink.

"You look beautiful, sweetie pie, and very French in that

lacy tee shirt you're wearing," he said. "I can't wait to see what's underneath it when we get to the house," he whispered as he nuzzled my ear, and I blushed. We loaded the car with his carry-on bag and a mysterious package—could it be a present— and suddenly we were on our way.

As usual, we talked and talked about Florida and home, our families, the state of our new French house. Sam knew that having gotten nowhere with Monsieur Hernandez or his inexperienced roofer, I had hired a mason to stop the leaks. His name was Jean Lafon, and he had done a lot of work around the village.

I took the A62 out of Toulouse and headed west and then north on the A20. Soon the city fell away, and in the distance, the colorful patchwork quilt of manicured fields unfurled before us, and we marveled at the beauty of the countryside, which looked just like a Bruegel painting. We passed road signs for other towns and villages. We followed the autoroute toward Bordeaux then north to Montauban, Caussade, until finally our exit appeared. My heart quickened, Sam squeezed my hand, and we exchanged a smile. Another *crunch* as I downshifted the gears at the turn off for Montpezat de Quercy and sped us home.

I couldn't wait to show Sam all the work I had done in his absence. As we entered the front door, he noticed the unusual niche in the wall and the colorful old tile floor in the entry.

"Gee, I don't remember this checkerboard tile pattern," he said. "It's unusual. I really like it."

"Yes," I agreed. "I wish these three tiles here weren't cracked. We'll never be able to find a match for this old pattern again to replace them."

I escorted Sam around to admire the improvements I had arranged in his absence. The plumber had installed a downstairs toilet. I had bought a new oven. The high courtyard walls were freshly whitewashed. Colorful geraniums, petunias and begonias were blooming in the front window boxes.

However, as I explained to him, the leaks in the attic were turning out to be a difficult problem to fix. The workman I had hired said that the source of the leaks was from the chimney on the party wall of the adjoining house to ours, which was owned by absentee owners who had basically abandoned their property. Monsieur Lafon, our mason, had no right to go on their roof to get to the root of the problem. All he could do was keep pouring cement on the place where the roofs of the two houses came together and hope that this would prove effective.

Nevertheless, the artisan was having an easier time working on the facade of the house and replacing the front windows and shutters. The place was going to look great when this was done. And hopefully be finished. Somehow our new house wasn't turning out to be as trouble free as we had thought. I should have known that old houses were like that. If it wasn't one thing, it was another.

There were a few odd jobs Sam was eager to dive into, but first came us and our time together. Sam loved to be busy, whether walking around an art gallery, a golf course, or his own home with a tool belt or a paint roller. The trick with him was to get the balance right.

I had purchased our new townhouse with the money from the sale of Pech Menal. Sam had promised to help me arrange the new place in Montpezat just as I liked, and I was looking forward to bringing my vision to fruition.

———

It was divine to awaken each morning to the sonorous bongs from the nearby church belltower, which chimed on the hour and the half hour. We were early risers, and seven bongs meant it was time to throw open the window shutters. Dust motes would sparkle like diamonds in the sunlight. When we leaned a little too dangerously out the window to check the weather, we could catch a glimpse of the church far below us and above it, the cloudless, bright, French blue sky. Summer felt endless. From our lofty bedroom window, we felt on top of the world.

Saint Martin's had been the village centrepiece for more than six hundred years. The *collégiale* bell tower was like another human presence in our lives. Instead of checking our cell phones or a clock, we could tell time by its bongs. We saw its 14th century southern Gothic-style silhouette day and night from our bedroom window, its red tile rooftop sparkling in the morning sunshine and bathed in moonlight at nighttime. The perky slope of its roof line was such an interesting shape, like an eyebrow shading mysterious openings that watched out toward the distant Pyrenees Mountains. The bell tower's proportions were so pleasing that we never got tired of looking at them. The church's massive stone bulk was like an anchor grounding us as we navigated our way through our initiation into the life of our French village.

Even though the building had suffered during the Hundred Years' War with the English and then again during two world wars, it still stood unbowed, watching over the valley. Sculptures were missing or broken in the niches of the facade, a stained-glass window had been destroyed, the richly embroidered vestments and gem-studded liturgical items for the Mass had been stolen or scattered. But Saint Martin's had prevailed. That was a lesson in endurance and perseverance that I would do well to apply in my own life.

But right now, it was time to wake up and smell the coffee, an American expression that Sam loved to repeat. Our bedroom was two flights up from the kitchen. Sam liked to descend the steep stairs to make our morning coffee, leaving me to luxuriate in bed like a princess, propped up on pillows counting my blessings to the huff and puff of the coffee machine downstairs. I loved this part of the day. The careful tread of Sam slowly ascending the stairs, carrying the small blue and orange Florentine tray, a *brocante* find. Carefully balanced on it would be my *bol* of *café au lait* and his mug, another second hand "gem," painted with a silly clown face with the word *Bonjour* spelled out in red letters.

We both loved the *brocante*, the local outdoor market where all kinds of trash and treasures from *les vides greniers,* the "empty your attics," was sold. Sam and I could spend hours happily wandering among the stalls before dropping into a café for a cup of coffee or perhaps a glass of wine. Our days were our own, and we intended to spend them leisurely.

Our mornings began with Sam crossing the street to buy croissants and a baguette at *dépôt de pain,* while I flung open the French doors to our courtyard to let the sunshine in and set the table for breakfast.

Across the narrow street, I could see our talkative, diminutive neighbor, Monsieur Meunier, watering the flowers that decorated his doorstep. He'd probably been up for hours, watching all the coming and goings, having casual conversations with passers-by. Nothing escaped him. That was how he knew everything that went on in our street, *la rue de la Libération,* named to commemorate France's freedom from the Nazi oppressors, and *not* as I sometimes liked to imagine for my own liberation from my marriage or from my job, or from my personal demons.

Our first morning together was spent strolling the town and greeting our new neighbors. Monsieur Meunier, whose house was kitty corner across the narrow street from ours, rushed to meet Sam.

Monsieur Meunier and I exchanged kisses in the French manner. Sam extended his hand and Monsieur Meunier shook it a bit awkwardly. *Le shake-hand* was not a French custom but a crazy Anglo-Saxon thing.

Monsieur Meunier's gaze dropped to Sam's naked ring finger. He was snooping, unsure of our marital status. He had nothing against cohabitation, but he was curious and liked to be in the know. As for Monsieur Meunier himself, he and his lady had lived together for many years without the benefit of clergy. These days such arrangements were very common, and even many young French people didn't bother to wed. It made the almost inevitable separation easier.

"Don't forget to water your window box flowers before the day gets too hot," Meunier instructed us. "Plants like to be watered early in the morning."

"Oui, oui," I said. "We'll take care of it right away. Have a great day."

Sam, sensing my desire to cut the conversation short, grabbed my elbow and guided me away with a friendly wave. "What was that all about?" he asked.

"Oh, Monsieur Meunier is always giving me advice," I explained. "He's a real nudnik. However, don't forget that he has a big vegetable garden and likes to give away zucchini when he's overloaded with them."

Next door to Monsieur Meunier was the *Boucherie*, which was permanently closed after the breakdown of the owners' marriage. Monsieur Delpech, the butcher, had moved out long ago. Madame Delpech still lived in an apartment above the shop. She was another chatterbox, but her favorite topic was herself, her latest operation, or how her husband was dragging out their divorce proceedings.

Sam and I passed by quickly. She seemed a little jealous of my handsome *mec,* and I knew she was observing us from her open balcony window as she chatted with a friend on the telephone.

We walked on and I observed our neighbor from the corner house, Mathieu. He was setting off on a morning walk with his signature jaunty air. He was head of the local hiking club and worked as a florist in Caussade, a nearby town. He was a very handsome man, in a Northern European way, all blonde hair and steely blue eyes. I had noticed him gallantly escorting a young woman into his house in the evenings or less gallantly showing one out early in the morning. I found him a little cold and hard to approach. I hoped that might change. After all, Sam and I were the newbies and friendships took time.

Some children passed us holding their mothers by the hand on their way to the elementary school at the end of the street. Their bell-like voices sounded so pretty, effortlessly emitting perfectly formed French sounds. Part way along they stopped by the newsstand, *la librairie-papeterie,* to beg their *mamans* for bon-bons, although they knew it was not allowed on a school day morning. The newsstand was run by the elderly Madame Longueville aided by her red-headed daughter, Karine.

Karine was already a friendly neighborhood acquaintance being young, charming, and full of pep. She stood out with her carrot red hair and asymmetrical haircut. She talked in a loud voice and laughed easily and often. A chain smoker, she was always trying to quit and then making a quick trip to Andorra to buy more cigarettes at tax-free prices. Aside from helping her mother, she gave private English lessons, but we always talked French together. Never a word of English. She waved her secateurs in greeting at us, then went back to deadheading the beautiful roses that grew outside her mother's premises. Heading towards her, no doubt with a conversation on gardening on her mind, was my friend Héloïse.

Héloïse Dutoit, a chic Parisian lady who arrived in the village not much before me, hadn't had an easy time. Her apartment had been in the tough Saint Denis neighborhood north of Paris where gangs ruled the streets, and the police feared to intervene. She and her daughter had had enough of feeling threatened and intimidated by the lack of law and order there, so they'd moved to Montpezat. The locals found her cool and aloof, which she was.

She had my understanding; I could see her reticence was just part of her big city ways. Thanks to her little poodle *Déesse,* she was already making some headway with the local dog walkers. They were a friendly group. She was too far away to call out to, plus Sam and I were intent on our morning walk and knew *Déesse* would slow us down with those little legs.

Chez Martine, the boutique on the corner with its carefully curated window, wasn't open this early in the morning, which was no surprise. The shop was owned by Martine and her sister Michou. They did not open until much later as both were so busy with the local markets at nearby towns, which they visited in Martine's huge motorhome stocked to the brim with clothing for men as well as women.

Finally, opposite *les Ursulines,* the 17th century convent that was now the school, was our other late opener, Michèle, *le coiffeur.* When she did arrive, she'd prop open her glass door covered with announcements for upcoming concerts, exhibitions, village fêtes and countless other activities. Michèle was on several town committees and was a mover and shaker in Montpezat.

Michèle and Martine were exceptions to the rule. Most people got an early start to the day because lunchtime would be upon them before they knew it.

The days were strictly divided into morning time, *le matin* from 8 to 12 o'clock, and *l'après-midi* from 2 o'clock until 6 in the evening, apéritif time, *l'apéro,* for short. From 12 p.m. until 2 p.m. it was lunchtime, which everyone took quite seriously. Stores were closed. Artisans went home to eat and take a break. The street emptied out completely and like its occupants, Montpezat fell into a quiet doze.

After our walk, Sam and I were going to take the car to Montauban to have lunch under the arcades of the beautiful Place Nationale. I wanted to show him how they had beautified the square even further while we had been away.

CHAPTER FOUR
MAKING NEW FRIENDS

Sonia Delaunay was fast becoming a recurring theme in my life that started with my visit to her wartime refuge at the nearby chateau de Grisolles and continued to my meeting with our new neighbor who, I would soon learn, actually owned a signed Delaunay painting.

I met Laure and her significant other one morning while crossing the *Place de la Résistance* on my way to the post office. They looked extremely chic in that classic style only the French can pull off and were standing in front of a medieval townhouse that had been abandoned for some time. Heads bowed close together, they spoke a low tone rapid-fire French. So not foreign buyers then. There were plenty of Danes and Brits who owned summer houses in Montpezat. The Frenchman was particularly elegant in khaki slacks, his off-white sweater slung over his shoulders, but his partner shone in what looked like a vintage Hermès blouse.

I circled around them not wishing to intrude when the toe of my sandal caught on a cobblestone. I took a nasty stumble and dropped the letters I was holding along with my dignity.

"Are you alright?" the woman called out. "Pierre-Paul, is *la petite dame* okay?" she asked her companion who was nearest to me.

Pierre-Paul came forward and scooped up my mail. "*Tout va bien, Madame?*" he asked solicitously.

"Honestly, I'm fine," I answered, a little flustered. "I was in a hurry to get to the post office before it closes for lunch and I tripped." I felt a little embarrassed, that was all.

My little embarrassment multiplied when Pierre-Paul handed back my envelopes and said, "Madame, *la poste* isn't open this morning. It's *mardi*. On Tuesdays, the post office is only open in the afternoon."

"*Oh là là,* so much for hurrying." I smiled ruefully. I hadn't yet learned all the intricacies of the opening and closing times of the businesses and services in the village. "*Je me présente,*" I pressed on, making the best of my clumsiness. "I'm Barbara Waldheim. I've just bought the house next to *Les Trois Terrasses,* the bed and breakfast in the *rue de la Libération.*"

"Ah ha," said the woman with delight. "You're *l'américaine,* I've heard about. I'm so happy to meet you. *Je m'appelle Laure Acosta-Moneda.*"

"*Enchantée.* Pleased to meet you." I thought Laure must be the redoubtable Parisian woman everyone talked about. Some people liked the Parisians who had second homes in the village, and some resented them a little. But since Laure and her family had been coming to Montpezat for many, many years, they were accepted as village fixtures.

"*Et je suis Pierre-Paul Archambault, un ami de Laure. Ravi de faire votre connaissance.*" Laure's elegant friend very politely introduced himself, declaring that he too, was pleased to meet me.

In her rapid fire, non-stop way of speaking, Laure then

launched into an explanation of why she and Pierre-Paul were standing in the square eyeing a wreck of a house. "I've just bought this old ruin next to my mother's holiday house. It needs almost a total rebuild. We were considering hiring Jean Lafon, the local mason to start working on it, but we've just received his *dévis,* the estimate. It's higher than expected."

"Funny, but I just hired Jean Lafon, the mason, to work on my house." Monsieur Lafon was working on fixing my leaky roof among other things.

"You did? *Quelle coïncidence!*" Pierre-Paul added. "You recommend him then?"

"I do. He's going to *ravaler la façade,* remove the cement covering from the front of my house to expose the old bricks and half-timbers of the original facade."

Laure exclaimed, "*Impeccable!* That's what I want to do too, after the inside of the place is put right. First things first. It turns out there is a layer of packed earth in between each of the floors which must be replaced. I can tell you that I have never run into anything like this where I live in Paris."

I was amused to learn that they, too, had house renovation problems, which we could bond over. "What? They used earth for insulation. You mean dirt, like soil?" I asked, clarifying that I understood correctly. I made a mental note for Monsieur Lafon to check out my floors and insulation.

Pierre-Paul gestured idly toward the house, his monogrammed pinkie ring sparkling in the sun. "Yes, years ago they insulated between the floors with dirt. It was their technique—the best they could do, I suppose. No fiberglass insulation back then. *Pas de lin de verre* in those days."

"*Barbara, es-tu libre, ce soir?* Are you free this evening? You must come over and have an *apéro* with us." She drawled out my name French style with equal stress on each syllable so that it came out *BAR-BAR-AH*.

"That would be lovely," I told her. "*Merci pour l'invitation. May I bring Sam? He's my copain,*" I said, using the French word used to describe my boyfriend, partner, lover, significant other, all in one.

"*Certainement.* Come over to *chez maman*, right next door." Laure pointed out the house. "That's where we're living for now until this one is habitable."

"*D'accord.* What time?"

"*Eh bien,* around six thirty," Laure specified with a Gallic shrug, as if it went without saying.

"*Impeccable,* See you this evening, then. We'll bring a bottle of rosé."

———

Laure and Pierre-Paul were good hosts. They wanted to know all about us in the nicest way. We ate and drank a tad too much, but the rounds of sausage that Laure and Pierre-Paul had just brought back from Spain and cubes of Basque cheese from the nearby Pyrenees were delicious.

Laure had prepared a goat cheese and tomato tart with a super thin crust. Pierre-Paul poured a hearty red wine from a new vineyard he had visited in the Lot, the next department north of the Tarn-et-Garonne toward Cahors.

After an hour or two, Sam and I left for home happy to have met such hospitable and delightful neighbors. From that first apéritif hour, our friendship grew by leaps and bounds.

Laure was an intellectual bluestocking, a former high school Spanish teacher, whose political leanings were very left wing. Pierre-Paul, on the other hand, former business executive that he was, had a much more conservative outlook on politics and current events. It looked like they had long ago agreed to disagree, and perhaps that was what made them such an intriguing couple to hang out with. They loved culture as much as they loved politics as much as they loved good food and wine and entertaining. Sam and I found them a joy to be around.

Once home, Sam and I excitedly climbed the stairs to our bedroom, still a bit tipsy.

"Look at how dark your arm is against my skin," I said, comparing our skin tones as we leaned companionably against each other on the pillows.

"That's because you are a pale white rose, and I am a swarthy Sarrazin pirate who is going to ravish you!" Sam growled into my ear, prickling my neck with his unshaven chin. No idle threat, the North African brigands had terrorized medieval Frenchman from the south even as fierce Norsemen raided from the north in their longboats.

"Stop, you're tickling me." I tried to wriggle away, laughing, but he grabbed me and pulled me closer for a kiss. Unabashed, Sam pulled his tee shirt over his head with a happy grin. His body was tanned and trim with, for my taste, just the right musculature from his gym workouts. His stomach was flat, with a trace of a six pack. He grabbed me in his embrace and kissed me deeply. I slipped off my nightie and settled into his arms.

———

In the days to follow, Laure took to popping over the short distance from her mother's place to mine at the drop of a hat. I'd make us espresso and we'd sit together at the high marble bar in my kitchen cum dining room cum living room. Or perhaps we would go to the *Café de l'Union* on the corner of the *Boulevard des Fossés,* where the old town moat used to be in medieval times before it was filled in. We'd sit on the terrace overlooking the valley talking and watching the passersby. Laure would drink her espresso coffee slowly, so it lasted a long time. This was an in-born French talent that I sorely lacked.

My coffee was finished in a few minutes. But I loved talking with Laure. I felt we had a real connection even if I sometimes had to barrel my way into her mile-a-minute conversation. If someone she knew came along, Laure would invite them to join us at the table. I met a lot of new people through her; she certainly helped Sam and me ease into our new neighborhood.

Sam and Pierre-Paul took to one another as well. It was a case of opposites attract. Pierre-Paul's manner was rather aristocratic and Sam, although very polite, was a working stiff. It helped that he liked to dress stylishly. Sam was always carefully attired; even when doing odd jobs around the house, he never looked sloppy.

Many an afternoon, the two guys drove off to explore the local vineyards and sample the wine. Sam listening hard to Pierre-Paul's beautiful French, as he explained grape, and acidities, and vintage, he'd nod along from time to time, intent on soaking all this precious information up. Later, he confided to me that he only understood a small percentage of what Pierre-Paul said, however, the Frenchman's goodwill and cheerful disposition, his *bonhomie,* needed no translation. And Sam surely liked wine and bought many a bottle on Pierre-Paul's recommendation.

One evening we were having an *apéro* at our house and talking about Laure and Pierre-Paul's renovations, which were proceeding slower than expected, as is usual with that sort of thing.

"Are you happy with Monsieur Lafon's recent work?" Pierre-Paul asked.

"Very much so," I said. "Come see. Let me give you the grand tour." And so, we all gamely clambered up the many stairs and Sam and I showed them the formal living room on the next floor up and the bedrooms and bathroom on the floor above that.

When we got to my art studio on the fourth floor, 'le 3e étage,' they wanted to see the paintings I had stacked up against the wall.

"Sure." I pulled a canvas into the light from the rooftop window, *la lucarne*. I was always pleased to show my work—pleased and apprehensive at the same time. It was a very personal thing. By chance, the first painting I pulled out was of the church in Montpezat, *la collégiale* Saint Martin, down the hill from me.

"Barbara, *je l'adore*," Laure exclaimed. "It's so free! Don't you love it, Pierre-Paul?" Laure asked her boyfriend in her signature enthusiastic style.

"*Oui, c'est beau*," said Pierre-Paul, "but let's see the others, *ma chérie*."

"*D'accord*, but doesn't this one of the *collégiale* remind you of my Marianne Von Werefkin painting?"

"The one you bought in Switzerland? Why, yes. Yes, indeed. It's the same kind of expressionist style. And of course, the same colorful treatment," Pierre-Paul said thoughtfully. He was also an amateur painter specializing in nautical themes and seascapes, which was logical because he was from Normandy.

"You bought a painting *en Suisse*, Laure? You must tell me about that. I'd love to see it sometime. Is it here in Montpezat?" The name Von Werefkin was unfamiliar to me. I'd have to ask my niece, Melanie. She was studying Art History at a university back home.

We were close and talked every weekend on the phone. In fact, Sam and I were delighted to have persuaded her to come visit us this summer or the following one.

"No, I don't keep it here. It's stored away with a Delaunay."

"Sonia Delaunay?" My ears perked up. Now there's a name that just kept popping up. I had just seen that exhibit about her. Before I could tell Laure about it, she abruptly changed the subject.

"*Oui*. I'll tell you all about it later," she told me coyly, and I let it go.

Feeling more at ease showing my canvases to my enthusiastic friends, I propped up my paintings, one after the other, so they could look at my *toiles*, my canvases. There were depictions of the sunflowers, the fields, the water tower at Montalzat, and the fountains at a chateau Sam and I had visited in Dordogne. My friends were generous with their praise, and I glowed with pleasure.

Laure and Pierre-Paul had to go, so we trotted back down the long staircase from floor to floor and Sam and I showed them out. Standing on the rug we had put in the entry to hide the pretty but cracked tiles, Sam waved them goodbye, *au revoir*, see you soon, as he closed the door.

CHAPTER FIVE

MELANIE, SONIA AND SOME NEW INFORMATION

I couldn't wait to call my niece Melanie and tell her my friend Laure was an art collector who owned works by famous women artists like Delaunay and Von Werefkin. Melanie was like the daughter I never had. She was my younger sister Amanda's daughter. She was a graduate student in Art History and the Practice of Art at the prestigious Ringling School of Art and Design in Sarasota, Florida, the town where Sam and I spent our winters. We got to see her quite a bit during the school year, although her course of study required her to do research at universities up north in New York and Philadelphia.

Her special area of concentration was photography, and she was a talented shutterbug. However, she was deeply knowledgeable about art and artists in general, and I loved going to galleries and museums with her where she enhanced my enjoyment of the exhibition with her erudite running commentary.

Sam and I had Melanie over for dinner often when we

were back in Florida. It wasn't so easy to prepare a meal for her since my niece was vegan and didn't eat any foods coming from animals including dairy products or eggs. When Melanie dined with us, I usually prepared a tabouli, and Sam made us one of his Italian ice concoctions for dessert.

Sam and I both enjoyed hearing about my niece's weekends spent clubbing and attending concerts. For all her intellectual rigor, Melanie was kind of a wild child. Her arms were covered with tattoos of flowering tropical vines and her earlobes were pierced three times each. Yet, a study in contradictions, Melanie was also *straight edge*, which meant that she did not use tobacco, drugs or alcohol. She even had a tattoo of three x's, the straight edge movement's symbol, on the inside of one wrist to remind her of her vow of abstinence.

My sister back in New Jersey found her strong-willed daughter a handful. Melanie and I, however, bonded over the arty side we had in common. It was Melanie who had sent the present Sam had brought with him on the plane. The box contained a framed photograph she had made for me to decorate the new house in Montpezat de Quercy. It was a kind of forerunner since she intended to come to visit us soon.

I stayed up past midnight to call Melanie on a weekday evening when she was likely to be home. We usually texted or emailed, but I wanted to talk to her in person.

"Melanie, it's Aunt Barbara," I said when the call went through. "How are you? I got your gift. The photograph is hanging above the sofa in the Montpezat house, here where I am sitting at this moment."

"Aunt Barbara! *Bonjour!*" Melanie cooed happily into the receiver, "or should I say *bon soir?* Hold on a minute. I'll just turn down the music so I can hear you better." After a beat, she continued. "Hi there. Did you like my present?"

"It's beautiful, Melanie, and unusual. Thank you again. The photo is very sophisticated and Parisian. Of course, here in Montpezat we are far from Paris, but listen, I have some exciting news about a famous Parisian artist and a friend of mine. I can't wait to tell you about it."

"Well...spill. You've piqued my curiosity."

I told her about my friend Laure and her Sonia Delaunay painting. "And I just saw a big exhibit about Delaunay near Montpezat. She actually hid out at a chateau near here in a village called Grisolles at the end of the war."

"Oh, that is interesting! I read something like that in a paper we were assigned recently for my course on Women Artists of the 20th Century." Melanie seemed to know a good deal about Sonia. She told me that Sonia Delaunay was the first living woman artist to have a retrospective exhibition at the Louvre Museum and that in 1974, the president of France made a gift of one of her paintings to America when he visited Washington, DC. "It's in the National Gallery."

"Really! That's very impressive."

We then discussed how Sonia and her second husband Robert were on the cutting edge of modern art in Paris before the First World War.

"The paper we read outlined how Madame Delaunay managed to reinvent herself after 1945 to become an art world darling once again," Melanie said.

"You know, Melanie, my friend, Laure, goes so far as to compare my artwork to another artist she owns, Marianne Von Werefkin. Who is she? Do you know?"

"Why, yes, I do know something about her. She's been newly rediscovered, so to speak. She was Lithuanian but lived and painted with her husband, a German expressionist painter in Munich and then in Switzerland. They were associated with the Blaue Reiter group of artists in the 1910s. Her work is now very sought after. It is very colorful and imaginative."

"Really," I said. "I'm in good company then. Laure has even bought a couple of my paintings," I reported proudly. "She says they remind her of Von Werefkin's but don't need to be insured."

"Good for you, Aunt Barbara. That is so nice! You and Sam are really making the right sort of artsy, supportive friends there in Montpezat."

"It's true that we are meeting lots of interesting people here in the village, from local farmers to furniture makers to winemakers to expat wine drinkers. I can't wait for you to visit. I think you would enjoy the relaxed lifestyle. There are lots of little museums and places of interest we can visit. And you can practice your French." My niece, like many liberal arts majors, was required to study a foreign language. Melanie had decided to continue with French since she had already studied it in high school and as an undergraduate.

I felt a little tug of homesickness as I hung up. Sam was already sleeping when I crawled into bed next to him. It was 2 a.m. in Montpezat de Quercy according to the bongs from the bell tower.

Before I turned off my iPhone, I noticed a message had come in. Melanie had already emailed me the Sonia Delaunay article. Tired as I was, I started to read and learned that Sonia had done an excellent job of promoting Robert's and her own artwork after the war. She had a lot of competition from other big-name artists for gallery shows and museum placements, but Sonia succeeded by ceaselessly networking at the many parties and art shows she attended. She was even in touch with the American dealers who became increasingly important on the art scene as the 1950s progressed.

Just before I nodded off, I read that Tristan Tzara, the poet friend who was hiding with her at the chateau de Grisolles, proposed to marry her so they could grow old together.

Sonia wasn't interested. She was having too much fun on her own.

CHAPTER SIX

A VISIT TO THE CRYPT

Sam and I thought it was about time we learned more about our village's most outstanding monument. We walked down the hill to Saint Martin church and joined the small group surrounding Monsieur Claude Bruneau, the town expert on the *collégiale*. We'd signed up for the tour at 4 p.m. and duly paid our 5 euros apiece at the Montpezat Tourist Office. Montpezat was not an especially touristy town, but it had a tourist office. The Tourist Office in Montpezat organized the visits to the collégiale, held exhibits of local artists, and sold the local wines to the tourists who did pass through.

We arrived a few minutes late. It was just after 4 p.m., *16h*, when we entered the double leather doors to the nave. The temperature dropped and the light was filtered through the beautiful stained-glass windows. All except for the one simple glass window that was much plainer than the others. It rather spoiled the effect for me.

"En retard," Monsieur Bruneau hissed at us. Crotchety, erudite Monsieur Bruneau was conducting the tour. First, he

explained to us why this church, the *collégiale Saint Martin,* was called a *collégiale.* "A *collégiale* is a church that was endowed by its founder so that masses could be sung for his soul by churchmen, called canons, for all eternity—or until the money ran out. In Montpezat, the canons lived in houses constructed for them behind the church, which are still there." Bruneau recommended we go look at them later.

Bruneau told us that this church was named for Saint Martin, as many churches in the area were, after Martin, a Roman legionnaire, had cut off a piece of his cloak and given it to a naked beggar so he could clothe himself. This first generous act set the soldier on a path to Christianity and eventually to sainthood.

"And now," our guide said with a flourish, "let us look at the tapestries, which recount the life of Saint Martin in ten decorative panels. They were made in Flanders in the 16th century to hang in this very church." He pressed a lever that withdrew the curtain covering the weavings surrounding the church altar as they had for 400 years, except for wartime when they were hidden for protection.

Our group let out some *oohs* and *ahs* of appreciation. We made a circuit of the apse, studying each tapestry in turn:

1. Legionnaire Martin sharing his cloak with a naked beggar.
2. Martin subduing some highwaymen robbers.
3. Martin curing a leper.
4. Martin tempted by horned demons but resisting.
5. Martin converting to Christianity.
6. Martin falling ill but nursed back to health by angels.

7. Martin ignoring the temptations of beastly devils
   and malicious gossips.
8. Martin studying scripture in a medieval library.
9. Martin becoming a bishop.
10. Martin's soul going directly to heaven to sit at
    God's right hand.

In the background of the tapestries, the weavers depicted the flora and fauna of a beautiful, mythical land based on the reality of life around them. Castle chamber interiors had arched alcoves with decorated tile floors and sumptuous hangings on the walls. In the far distance, we saw the castle turrets shining on high hills where peasants brought in the bounteous crops, all beautifully depicted in thread.

When our time was up with the tapestries, Monsieur Bruneau expounded upon the collégiale's history and architecture and showed us the two *gisants*, recumbent statues, lying full length on either side of the nave near the altar. These life-size coffin cases showed the founder of the church and his nephew.

The founder was the vice-chancellor of the Roman church in Avignon, the fabulously wealthy Cardinal Pierre des Près. He gave the money to build and endow the church in the 14th century. His descendant, Bishop of Montauban, commissioned the series of tapestries for the altar in the 16th century. Between the two of them, they had created an attraction that still drew people to Montpezat de Quercy in the present day.

The sunlight streamed through the stained-glass windows high above the church aisle, creating a rainbow of brilliant colors on one of the stone columns holding up the ark-shaped roof of the house of worship. It was lovely to see red, yellow and blue reflections shining on the grey stone except for the window in the side chapel that was clear glass.

"Monsieur Bruneau," I piped up, "why doesn't that one window in the baroque chapel have stained glass? Its glass is so plain. Doesn't that rather spoil the effect?"

Bruneau didn't miss a beat answering my question, which had probably been asked many times before.

"The glass treatment in the window you are referring to is called *grisaille,* which means black and white or grey. It is a legitimate artistic concept often used in Italian Renaissance art to contrast some artwork with the full color renderings of most frescoes.

In our church setting here, the 19th century stained-glass window was destroyed in World War II and replaced by this simpler window of *grisaille* glass.

"What a shame!" I couldn't help but say aloud. Sam shushed me but it was too late. Bruneau swiveled in my direction.

"A shame!" Monsieur Bruneau epostulated. "Why the windows in this church are not the important features. You should be focusing on the fabulous tapestries and other treasures in the showcases set in the walls around the nave, which survived 600 years of history so that you could gaze on them today. It is only natural that there would have been damage and losses over the centuries to such an ancient monument as the collégiale de Saint Martin. What is incredible is that so much survived down to our era. That is what you should focus on. The church of Saint Martin was once enormously rich. After wars, pillaging and all sorts of depredations, these are the precious remnants that give an idea of the collegiale's former magnificence."

Bruneau continued. He was in full flood now.

"We've found traces of painted decoration on the walls and pillars of the church. It was not always the bare stone we associate with a typical church interior." Look over there," and he pointed. "You see the colors cast on the wall on your right. It's the sunlight reflections passing through the stained-glass windows. To medieval churchgoers, that jewel-like effect must have seemed like magic, colorizing the church stonework and sculptures. After all, in the Middle Ages people's lives were drab. Anything brightly colored was a rarity, like a precious stone. Colorful clothes were for nobility. Dyes, like blue *pastel*, were expensive. Only the very wealthy ever saw a book illustration, a precious hand-drawn illumination. For the illiterate public of those days, the whole church served as an encyclopedia of religious stories and parables—a kind of bible in stone, if you will. And when the sun cast stained-glass colors onto the church walls and floor, it must have seemed wondrous to the common people of the time. The colors must have seemed to them as if God himself had miraculously entered the church."

I'd never considered this idea. How true. Bruneau might not be the friendliest sort, but he certainly knew his stuff. It probably wasn't so easy regaling ignorant tourists with his hard-won knowledge week after week, year after year. This could explain Bruneau's impatience with a lot of questions and his touchy attitude. He felt proprietary about his church and his tapestries.

"And that concludes the visit for today," he announced. "My son, who is a director of the *Monuments Historiques de France* antiquities department, has written a monograph describing their recent excavations into the crypt of the *collégiale.* You can read about this latest research online, if you are interested. His name is Frédéric Bruneau." He seemed justifiably proud of his son. He had followed in his footsteps, so to speak. The *collégiale* seemed to be a Bruneau family affair.

"*Au revoir, messieurs-dames.* Feel free to stay a while longer in the church on your own." He headed down to the huge double doors.

"Sam," I said, "let's check out the *les vitrines* Bruneau mentioned."

"Sure. Might as well as long as we're here." There were six glass display cabinets, and we went around the church, peering at each one in turn.

"Nothing too impressive here," Sam said.

"Yes, but so old. To think these fancy little coffers have survived down to our era. The tag says they are from the 15th century."

"Hey, did you see this alabaster carving? I love this sculpture."

I was looking at a small plaque which was labeled *the Ascension of Christ, 14th century.* It showed mourners gathered around an open coffin. Right above it, a figure's legs and feet were visible ascending up a kind of laundry chute. It was Jesus depicted rising to heaven like a reverse Santa Claus going up the chimney. Its naïveté was very appealing.

"I love it," I said again. "But I still don't like the plain black and white window in this chapel."

Sam laughed. "You made that quite clear, my dear. Barbara, I'm ready for a change of scene. Let's go have an *apéro* at the café."

I agreed. We walked up the hill back toward our house and the Café de Union.

———

Later that week, Sam was flying to Israel to see his family in Tel Aviv, taking advantage of the shorter trip there from France as opposed to from Florida. I would miss him, but the good news was I now had a chance to catch up with acquaintances who were more my friends than his. I called Héloïse, whom I hadn't seen for some time. She'd been busy assisting her older neighbor, Didier Tarbarly. Didier was an ex-mayor of Montpezat and had fallen very ill. Heloise was helping him convalesce. I was particularly glad she was free for a night out at the cinema.

The next evening, I was driving us both back from Caussade, which has the nearest movie theatre. We had just seen the latest Pedro Almodovar film and we were discussing Penelope Cruz's performance when Héloïse suddenly announced, "Barbara, I have something to tell you that is upsetting me."

I knew something had been needling her lately. "What's the matter?"

"People are talking—*les commères, les mauvaises langues,* the gossips. They're spreading rumors behind my back."

"Is that so? I haven't heard anything. What's going on?" I was intrigued and a little annoyed for my friend. She seemed very put out and a little embarrassed.

"You know about my friend, Didier. He was once mayor of Montpezat. He was a good mayor, dedicated to his job. His wife died long ago, and they never had children. He isn't in good health, and I'm helping him out now. I'm visiting him, bringing him groceries, keeping him company from time to time."

"Of course, but what's wrong with that?" I asked. "It's very nice of you, Héloïse."

"*Effectivement,* Barbara. But the gossips say that I'm only after his money. They say that my behavior is inappropriate and self-interested. That I've cast a spell on him." Héloïse unstiffened for a moment and her expression softened. "And you know, I like Didier. I really like him. He's a nice old gentleman. He was once an important personage in Montpezat. And if he's attracted to me, can I help it?" she finished, perhaps a little proudly.

I felt sympathy for Héloïse as I steered the Citroën around the curvy departmental road up the hill back to Montpezat. She was a newcomer to Montpezat like me and was just trying to keep her head above water and get her teenage daughter settled in.

"No worries, Héloïse," I assured her. "*Ne t'inquiète pas.* I haven't heard anything negative about you, and I certainly won't be taken in by spiteful rumors if I do hear any."

She seemed calmed down by my words. To take her mind off things, I thought to tell her the news that an acquaintance from Montpezat, my friend, Laure Acosta-Moneda, was the owner of a painting by a famous artist. I asked her if she'd heard of Sonia Delaunay, the abstract painter.

Héloïse thought the name might ring a bell from an art history class she'd once taken.

To distract her further from her problems, I asked her about her daughter, who, like her mother, struggled with their new environment. "How is Colette?" I asked.

"She's taken up a class in cartooning," Héloïse said brightly. "Not what I expected, but she is much happier and meeting more young people like herself." She shrugged. "I am not complaining."

"That's wonderful! Did I tell you my niece is coming out for a visit sometime. We should get the two of them together."

We continued chatting about family until we arrived back in the village. I dropped Héloïse off at the end of the impasse that led to her little apartment, waved goodbye, and then I continued home.

———

A few days later I met Héloïse out walking her dog. She gave me a big smile and slowed down to talk with me. She was looking fine, carefully coiffed, wearing well-pressed chinos, which showed off her long legs.

"Barbara, nice to see you. I have some news. First, Didier is in the nursing home now."

"*Désolée*, Heloise. I'm sorry to hear that."

"Better for me," she replied. "It's easier. There's more help."

"I see." It made sense. Héloïse could only do so much as Didier deteriorated.

"You'll be interested to know," she continued, "that when I told Didier about your friend in the village who owns a Sonia Delaunay, he was very excited. He said that while he was town mayor, Madame Delaunay was commissioned to design a modern artwork to decorate the *collégiale* in Montpezat. Didier says that the French Minister of Culture arranged for her to create the work for the church of Saint Martin.

"No way!" I gasped. "Here! In Montpezat de Quercy?" Privately I was astonished at another instance where Sonia Delaunay's name had come up. I seemed to have conjured her into my life and my village.

"*Mais oui*. It was very in vogue at that time in the 1960s to engage famous artists to decorate cultural monuments. Soulages, the artist who is famous for works in black, did the abbey of Conques. Marc Chagall painted the Opera Garnier ceiling in Paris."

"But...but..." I was thunderstruck. "But where is the Sonia Delaunay artwork? I never saw anything like that in the *collégiale*."

"I know," she agreed. "*Moi non plus*. Didier didn't know what became of the artwork. It's mysterious. I pressed him on it. He was very sure of the basic facts. You see, Didier was such an intelligent, authoritative man. And he still is... but he's quite ill. I'm not sure he will last much longer."

"I'm sorry to hear that, Héloïse." I said sincerely. I didn't know Didier at all. He had been mayor many years ago. He had lived a long life after his term in office and most people had forgotten him. "And thanks for filling me in about Sonia Delaunay. What an astonishing development," I told her.

I wondered if this news had anything to do with the months Madame Delaunay spent hiding in Grisolles.

"*Au revoir*." We went our separate ways.

My mind was whirling trying to imagine a bold, colorful, very abstract Sonia Delaunay artwork hidden away in the village's 14th century southern Gothic-style church somewhere. This was an amazing piece of news. I couldn't wait to share it with Laure.

Héloïse continued down the street towards the *médiathèque*, the library, with her dog. I had been on my way to the '*Huit à Huit*' grocery store. It wasn't *really* open from 8 a.m to 8 p.m. It closed for two hours at lunch like everywhere else, but it was a catchy name.

I immediately changed my trajectory. Instead of going to the *Huit à Huit*, I stopped by Laure's house to see if she was at home, and I was in luck. Over a cup of tea out on her *terrasse*, I excitedly imparted my big news.

"Laure," I launched right in, "did you know that Sonia Delaunay once made an artwork to decorate the collégiale Saint Martin. Héloïse Dutoit, the new woman in town, is very close to former mayor Tabarly. He told her that when he was mayor in the nineteen sixties, she got a commission to make a decoration for the church here."

Laure's face went through a succession of expressions from surprise to scepticism to cautious excitement. "Really? That's news to me. I know Delaunay lived and worked in Paris. In my mind, she is always associated with Paris, not the Tarn-et-Garonne."

"Yes, but the other day when I went to pick up Sam when his flight got delayed, I spent an hour at the chateau de Grisolles. There was an exhibition there about artists who hid in Grisolles during the war. And Sonia Delaunay was one of them, at least for the last months of 1944."

"Really? That is very surprising to me. But still, there is no Delaunay artwork in the collégiale. Have you visited Saint Martin's? Even if Mayor Tabarly's memory is correct, nothing ever came of such a piece of art. It doesn't exist."

Stymied, we both sat sipping our tea. "Tell me about the Delaunay painting you bought in Switzerland. May I see it? Is it here in Montpezat or at your apartment in Paris?" She had promised to tell me the details sometime.

"The painting isn't hanging here or at my apartment in Paris where you can see it because..." Laure hesitated. She bit into a little *petit beurre* biscuit. A couple of seconds passed by. "Barbara, it's like this," she said finally. "I own a couple of paintings that are too valuable to hang at home. I don't display them. They are kept in secure, climate-controlled conditions in

Geneva when they are not out on loan to museum exhibitions."

"Oh my." I waited for what might follow.

The dam broke. "You might as well know the whole story," Laure went on. "One afternoon a few years ago, I got a call from a lawyer asking me if I was Laure Kieffer. That's *mon nom de jeune fille*, my maiden name. The lawyer explained that he had been hired on behalf of the giant Swiss bank, UBS, to search for the next of kin of Monsieur Henri Kieffer. Henri Kieffer was my long lost, unmarried uncle who had emigrated to New York in the 1920s. I knew very little about him. The lawyer told me that he had founded a bank in the United States before he got disillusioned with America and returned to Europe. He had died childless, *sans descendance*."

"Ok," I said softly. *"Et alors?"*

"Well, the lawyer also tracked down my brother and our elderly cousin. It seemed that Uncle Henri's little bank had somehow over the years been absorbed by UBS, the giant Swiss banking conglomerate. Now that he had died, UBS wanted to divest themselves of any liability they might have to his heirs by paying them off for his shares which had accrued considerable value."

Laure looked at me questioningly.

I waited, rapt, hanging on to every word for her to continue.

"So, there I was, a rather humble Spanish teacher at my Paris *lycée,*" she said, "well-educated, but not particularly affluent, suddenly an heiress with numbered Swiss bank accounts in Geneva!"

"Laure, that's amazing! You must have been bowled over," I exclaimed.

"The inheritance changed my life alright," Laure told me. "It was kind of hard to get used to and fantastic all at once. But

I haven't told you about the artwork yet. My Swiss financial advisors counseled that I should invest some of my newfound wealth in art. And of course, since I love art, that idea was very appealing to me. I wanted to support women artists, which it turned out was also a good investment idea.

"So, I went to galleries and bought the Marianne Von Werefkin painting. But the jewel of my collection is a very fine painting by the French artist, Sonia Delaunay, which I was extremely lucky to acquire at auction."

This story impressed me mightily. I had never known someone who owned art valuable enough to be on loan to museums. And Laure was so down to earth and friendly. True, she did sometimes behave in a peremptory manner and Pierre-Paul's nickname for her was *la baronne*. I guess this explained it.

"Bar-ba-rah," Laure announced. "We should investigate this matter. Wouldn't it be wonderful if Montpezat de Quercy had a Sonia Delaunay? A modern artwork like that in addition to the 16th century tapestries would put our village on the map and assure its continued prosperity."

"Well, what do you propose that we do?" I asked her.

"Let me think it over and talk to Pierre-Paul. We'll map out a plan of action."

"*Entendu*," I agreed. I wanted to tell Sam about it, too, which I did in my very next phone call to him in Israel.

"Sonia Delaunay," Sam repeated. "The lady who painted the colorful circles? Weren't she and her husband among the founders of modern art? They're right up there with Picasso and Matisse and Braque. Chagall, Léger, all of them." Sam often amazed me with his knowledge of art and music.

"Sonia Delaunay," I echoed him. "That's what I was told. I called Melanie in Florida to tell her the news and ask her what she thought of the possibility that Sonia Delaunay made an artwork for the *collégiale* back in the 1960s. She felt it could well be possible. We've got to follow up on this, Sam. We can't just let it go, can we?"

"Absolutely not, Barbara. Let's talk to Laure about it as soon as I return."

———

By the time Sam returned to Montpezat from Israel, Héloïse Dutoit was the talk of the village. Didier Tabarly had died. He had made Héloïse his heir *en viager*. This meant that in exchange for her caring for him for the remainder of his life, should it be long or short, she would inherit his property. In this case, a lovely house across from the *Huit à Huit*.

People said that the ink was hardly dry on the *viager* agreement when he died. People were outraged. People were jealous as if Héloïse, an outsider, had gotten away with something underhand. There was going to be an investigation to make sure that she had not hastened the ex-mayor's death to get her hands on his property. The French government would make sure that there had been no foul play given the short time frame between Héloïse's *viager* agreement and Didier's death.

"I haven't seen Héloïse around," Sam said to me.

"I talked to her on the phone and she's keeping a low profile these days," I told him, thinking of my poor, maligned friend. I had kept in touch to try and boost her spirits, but Heloise was as pragmatic as ever.

"It will all blow over," she said, "and someone or something new will grab the gossips' attention."

And she was right, but little did I know Sam and I would be at the center of the new thing or things—discoveries that would rattle the old stones of the entire village. I reached up to touch the new haircut Michèle the coiffeur had just given me. I hoped it wouldn't be flattened by the detective's cap I would soon be wearing.

Sam and I didn't have a pet. Neither did Laure and Pierre-Paul. We'd have to be our own bloodhounds.

CHAPTER SEVEN

SEARCHING FOR THE MISSING ARTWORK

Our friend and neighbor, Laure, had thought things over. She was on board with us to investigate the disappearance of the artwork Sonia Delaunay created for la *collégiale Saint Martin*. The quest appealed to her on several levels.

First, she owned a Delaunay painting and was already an admirer of the artist. Second, her family had long considered Montpezat de Quercy their second home so she would be only too happy to add another feather to the village cap, so to speak. With a modern artwork by a lauded artist in addition to the church's collection of medieval tapestries, the *collégiale* would be a Michelin-starred attraction listed in all the guidebooks. Montpezat's cultural clout would be assured.

The problem was that the trail had gone stone cold. Hard evidence was scarce. Didier Tarbarly, the former mayor and benefactor of my friend, Héloïse, had died leaving his firm insistence that such an artwork was indeed commissioned during his time in office. However, neither the present mayor nor his predecessor had any knowledge of a Delaunay work.

Laure and Pierre-Paul had checked it out at the town hall and drawn a blank. The present occupants of *la Mairie,* weren't any help. There were no records to be found of a gift to the *collégiale* from Madame Delaunay. Brigitte, Monsieur *le Maire's* right-hand woman, and de facto head administrator of the town for many years, was *catégorique.* She didn't know anything about a Delaunay decoration created for the church of Saint Martin.

Laure felt the next angle was to approach our local church officials. I was elected to talk to *monsieur le curé, le père* Rossignol whom I already knew. The good Father and I shared a love of word games. He liked to do the jumble word puzzles in the *International Herald Tribune* to which he had a subscription. Since I loved the crosswords, he would drop the folded newspaper behind the flower boxes on my front windowsill when he had finished with the *Jumble,* so that I could do the weekly crossword. This arrangement was loosely predicated on me attending Sunday services from time to time, a good deal from my point of view, and typical of my quirky life in rural France.

I'd originally met the priest the previous summer at the Feast of St. Jean, the festival that celebrates the start of summer with a huge party and a bonfire. *Le père* was there to bestow Christian blessings on the pagan affair. His participation was much appreciated as he was a popular figure with the villagers.

Courtly Father Rossignol had been born and bred in Montpezat de Quercy. During his career, he'd spent many years at a senior level in the Vatican and returned to Montpezat on his retirement. Still a very handsome man despite his ninety years, he was ruddy and well-built with broad shoulders. He liked to hike, a popular pastime in Montpezat, which added to his being a favorite with the village.

He'd noticed me, the anglophone newcomer at the festival, and cordially introduced himself to me with his excellent Italian-accented English from his time at the Vatican. Our friendship had developed from then on. Unfortunately, *Père* Rossignol was no help with the Sonia Delaunay mystery. He had never heard a whisper of any such artistic donation to the *collégiale,* which only deepened the mystery, as surely someone of his status would have heard something?

That left the town expert on the *collégiale,* the formidable Monsieur Bruneau, and he'd be the hardest nut to crack for sure.

He'd hate that there was anything to do with his church that he didn't know about. This could easily be taken as a personal insult, if he chose to see it like that. It was therefore decided that Laure take the lead in these discussions, and despite her best efforts, she didn't get very far with him.

First, he explained, any such artistic commission would have been in his father's time, not his. His father had been the collégiale expert before him. Secondly, he himself was opposed in principle to the idea of mixing a modern artwork with the medieval church decoration. How would it accord with the beautiful and elaborate 16th century tapestries? It would be a travesty in his opinion.

We'd suspected this might be the way things would go, but Laure persisted.

"*Mais oui,* Monsieur Bruneau, but there must be some trace of this artwork. It would have been *très important.* It can't have just vanished into thin air! It must be stored somewhere. It can't have been simply lost."

Or stolen? Like Laure, I too was beginning to have suspicions about the matter. Costly artworks donated on a bureaucratic level shouldn't just disappear.

"What exactly are you talking about anyway, Madame Acosta-Moneda? A tapestry? A painting? It is all so vague," he said sniffily. His lack of interest becoming apparent.

Undeterred, Laure forged on. "You tell me, Monsieur Bruneau. Where would such an object have been put to be kept safe? If it's not in the church proper or the canons' houses behind the church, could it be in the crypt?"

This was daring of Laure, the crypt was the sacred purview of Bruneau's son, Frédéric, who was making a name for himself with *les Monuments Historiques de France,* publishing monographs on the painstaking investigation of the tombs that lay underneath the church.

"Hah! And you think this unspecified whatever of a non-existent artwork might be in the crypt! Did you ever consider that maybe this artwork never got created at all?" Bruneau snorted. "I will see what Frédéric says about all this nonsense." This was said mostly to get rid of us, but Bruneau kept to his word and agreed to deputize his son, Frédéric, to let us into the *collégiale's* crypt to look around. This was a great honor and a concession.

Luckily, Frederic was intrigued and had a slightly different outlook from his father. And so, we three found ourselves deep under the church apse peering around in the semi-darkness while Frédéric shared some of his special knowledge of medieval church crypts in layman's terms.

"In the early days of the Catholic church, services were often conducted in secret. Underground sanctuaries were the safest places for worshippers and for safeguarding the bones and other precious relics brought back from the crusades, for example. The tombs of founding priests and important converts could also be protected. Hence crypts. Crypt means dark in Latin. Like the word, cryptic, as in hard to see or understand.

As the Catholic faith became predominant, there was no longer any reason to hide in darkness. By the 13th and 14th centuries, airy, vaulted constructions, marvels of medieval engineering, were built over the crypt—the buildings which we now call churches. Like St Martin's," he said. "You probably have noticed that while the church's arches are pointed, or Gothic, down here the earlier arches that support the crypt roof crypt are rounded, or Romanesque."

I hadn't, to be honest. Frédéric was obviously passionate about his work and very good at communicating his interests. I was glad that, unlike Bruneau Senior, he seemed to have an open mind about the Delaunay work. At least his curiosity was piqued.

"If you care to look down you will see we are now walking on tombstones," he continued as we stumbled through the gloom. Sure enough, the floor was made of incised coffin covers showing the dim outline of medieval knights and prelates. Set into the walls between the squat pillars were sarcophagi. Some had Latin inscriptions. Some had sections of carving that had been repurposed from earlier Roman coffins.

"This is fascinating," Sam said. "Who is the imposing figure carved on this coffin here, Frédéric? Do you know?"

"Aha," said Frédéric. "Good question. We think that is one of the relatives of the des Près family. You will recall that it was Pierre des Près who founded the *collégiale* in the 1300s. He became fabulously rich in the service of his friend, Jacques Duèze, who went on to become Pope Jean XXII. Des Près was his lawyer and financial advisor. He must have given very good financial advice indeed because they both became immensely wealthy. This was during the time of the church schism when there were two Popes, one in the Vatican in Rome and one in Avignon where Pope Jean held his Papal court." Fred continued, impassioned by his subject, "I feel that this carving shows direct influence of the Avignon school. Notice the cut of the marble draperies here and the headdress on the figure. Proving this correlation is the focus of my most recent paper."

I was listening but also peering into the gloomier corners. "What are these excavations over here?" I asked, moving deeper into a low-ceilinged side chamber.

"Be careful, Madame! *Attention!*" Frédéric shouted at me.

I froze as if in a minefield.

"Don't cross those lines there," he said, pointing to some stakes in the ground. "We are excavating, hoping to find even earlier remnants from the Gallo-Roman or Merovingian eras."

"Okay." I stumbled backwards to the main group. "Those crates," I pointed at the packaging crates stored in the forbidden room. "Is that equipment for the dig?"

"Yes. Technical equipment. There are so many important crypts and archaeological sites in France that I must compete for the funding needed to carefully measure, document, and photograph everything. I keep these specialized tools and paraphernalia here at the ready for when I get a government grant.

Laure asked, "Frédéric, I've heard there are tunnels leading from the *collégiale* to the town. Have you found any evidence of these subterranean passages?"

"It is likely there are tunnels here in Montpezat waiting to be discovered. We have found the start of what might be a tunnel connecting the *collégiale* to the ancient hospice up the hill. It is now *les Trois Terrasses*, the fancy *chambre d'hôtes*."

"Wow!" *That was right next to my house!* I considered the distance up the steep hill and the logistics of constructing such an underground passageway.

"Look behind this pillar, see the steps." Frederic led us to a shadowy corner. "Take a further look down there, if you want, but be careful."

Sam led the way, and we crept, heads bent, along a dark passage, lighting our way with our cell phones. It was claustrophobic. We seemed to be descending farther below ground, not heading upward as I would have expected if this tunnel were to lead to the old town.

Something rustled and brushed by my head. I shrieked, "What was that?"

"*Beurk,* cobwebs!" cried Laure and got a mouthful of the filmy substance. "That means spiders. Hundreds of them. Let's get out of here!" she said. We had reached as far as we could go; a collapsed wall blocked our progress. Looking at the massive pile of stone rubble, suddenly it didn't feel too safe underground anymore.

We scrabbled back to the crypt proper where Frédéric was waiting for us with a sly grin on his face. "So, you went exploring, *oui?* Did you find any bats?"

"Bats, no. A lot of spiders, though," I said energetically dusting myself off. "They give me the creeps."

"See if any are on me," Laure twisted her back to me. "I feel as if spiders are crawling all over me."

"You're fine," I reassured her. "Frédéric sure has a funny sense of humor."

"Now you have a sense of the scale of my work down here," he said. We all climbed the steps up into the bright light of the apse. As the men walked on ahead, Laure and I followed, engrossed in a murmured conversation.

"I am disappointed we saw no trace of Sonia," Laure said.

"To be frank, I'm almost relieved. There's no way anything could still be down there and be in one piece."

Laure gave a typical Gallic shrug. "And those stones have

obviously collapsed longer ago than the sixties when the work would have been deposited."

"So, it's not in the crypt then," I said. "Where else could it be?"

"I'm afraid, my friend, that Sonia's work didn't make it this far," Laure said, looking downcast. "If she is anywhere, it is probably a private collection."

"You mean the piece, whatever it is, could have been stolen?" I had my own fears on this very subject.

"*Mais oui,*" Laure put on her sunglasses as we entered a bright French morning, so much sweeter after the dankness of the crypt. "We have checked with the bureaucratic and the ecclesiastical authorities and no one has heard of her. And the ex-mayor is no longer here to guide us. So, either he was mistaken, or someone has pulled a quick one; either way I fear we are at an impasse."

We bid farewell to Frédéric and thanked him for his tour. I pulled on my own sunglasses and together we stepped out and started up the hill home.

CHAPTER EIGHT
MORE HOUSE RENOVATION WOES

Laure, Pierre-Paul, Sam, and I let our Sonia Delaunay investigations drop, accepting it was all based on the hearsay of a dying man, and just one of those exciting ideas that are fun to follow for a while, but eventually fall by the wayside. Besides which, we were all preoccupied by house renovations for the time being.

Laure Acosta-Moneda's house on the square was coming along nicely. It was being fitted out with a new staircase made by the village furniture maker, a real craftsman of an *ébéniste*. He was also going to make her some custom kitchen cabinets, but first the walls had to be prepared and painted. So, one step at a time, but the work was progressing, and Laure was pleased.

What wasn't so pleasing to either of us was Monsieur Jean Lafon, the mason.

Laure had eventually fired him. He'd been working on the exterior of her house but more frequently distracted off the job and taking nips from a bottle he kept in his pocket. '*Il picolait,*' as they said around town, making a hand motion with the thumb tilting toward the mouth. In other words, he drank.

Sam and I had suspected as much. We weren't entirely satisfied with Lafon's work on our house either. He had removed the stucco treatment from our facade as agreed and exposed the pretty old stones, bricks, and half-timbers. But the new double-glazed windows on the street side were poorly installed and the shutters were hard to manoeuvre.

Furthermore, despite all the cement he had poured over the two party-wall roofs, between ours and our neighbor's house, leaks persisted. He claimed that the problem was related to the wall in that funny old alcove by the front door, but we couldn't see how, as it was clear on the other side of the house from the leaks in the attic. Thankfully, aside from the occasional passing thundershower, it didn't rain much in Montpezat and so the roof didn't leak much.

Sam and I had a new mantra now, *Ah well, the house has stood for 600 years and will likely stand for 600 more.* Or would it?

———

Meanwhile, a deep house cleaning was on the agenda. I was vacuuming the floor near the front door in the oddly recessed alcove area. Pieces of grit and leaves tended to collect there, and as I moved the vacuum up the stone wall behind a tapestry hanging – the one with the scene of the country wedding party I had bought from Monsieur Hernandez, I was thinking to myself that Sonia Delaunay had made a lot of fabric art, including tapestries.

Maybe that was why she had been chosen to make something for the Montpezat collégiale. The 14th century church was a fine example of its kind, and the canons' houses behind the church were beautiful and unusual. But it was the church tapestries that were exceptional. Their survival was an achievement, in that they still hung in situ in the very place they had been conceived for and had not disappeared or been lost.

Maybe the French Ministry of Culture had seen a correspondence between the medieval tapestries and Sonia's work as a fabric artist. Perhaps she might have made something out of fabric, which could be folded up and stuffed into a box any old place. It would be impossible to unearth; it could be in somebody's attic.

Sam came clattering down the stairs just then and I pounced. "Well, hi there. Can you help me with this, please? I want to get some of the cobwebs out from between the stones in this wall. If I hold up the tapestry out from the wall, can you reach the higher parts I can't?"

"Sure," Sam said agreeably. He was excellent at lending a hand. "Gimme the long nozzle."

He changed the vacuum head for the brush attachment. "Better still, if we take down the tapestry we can do a more thorough job."

"Ok, sure," I said. I took hold of my side of the pole, and we lay the heavy tapestry carefully onto the bright colored tile floor of the alcove.

Sam got to work, but when he finished and turned off the noisy vacuum cleaner, he said, "Barbara, what do you think these fibers are? They're sticking out through the mortar in between the stones?"

I took a good hard look, my nose inches from the wall. "I don't know, Sam. Maybe they mixed grass or horsehair into the mortar in olden times? Pierre-Paul told me something about it." I shrugged. "It's nothing."

"Maybe so," Sam said. "But this stuff seems to be more like

strings, although it is vegetal." He broke a strand off from the wall. He stroked the hairlike fiber with his fingers, considering it. "Barbara, you know, I think these are roots. There are roots growing in the wall here." His voice was pensive. "And they're wet! Is this part of the problem the mason was trying to explain?" Sam exclaimed.

"Nonsense." I switched on the flashlight on my phone and we both examined the offending fiber. Then I raised the light to the wall. It was riddled with hairy growths. "*Mon Dieu!* Where are these roots coming from?"

We traced them down to the floor where we noticed that there were more fine growths undermining the pretty tile work we liked so much in the front hall. *Why had we never inspected this area behind the front door more carefully?*

"Oh no," I lamented. "How could I have overlooked these growths! The light is so poor here that I never even noticed this problem. Ooh! It's creepy! It's like mysterious tendrils sprouting up from an underground world hidden beneath our tile floor."

"Where could all this be coming from? Sam asked.

"Next door!" We spoke in unison, shocked to think these growths might originate from *Les Trois Terrasses, la chambre d'hôtes* right next door.

We went straight out into the street to the gates of the *Trois Terrasses* and peered through the iron bars across the courtyard toward the side wall of our house. Right by the corner where our wall intersected with the courtyard was a little tree growing by an old well. It was all very picturesque.

"Could it be that tree?" I asked. "But it's a lovely tree. It blooms so prettily in the spring."

"Barbara, it's a Judas tree," Sam said. "It's aptly named.

That thing is undermining the wall and floor of the entry to our house."

The gate was locked so we couldn't go in, but upon further investigation, we learned that this innocuous little *arbre de Judas* was getting nourishment from the newly installed sewage system buried in the sidewalk next to our front door. The tree's roots had grown fast, thriving on access to both water and 'fertilizer' from the sewer. Somehow, they were leaking liquid into our wall.

We got the water company, *la Saur,* to come and open the sewer cover. When we all peered inside, Sam, me, and the water company workmen, we must have made an intriguing sight for Monsieur Meunier. He was hanging around his front door, hoping to be included.

Inside the sewer access the pipes were covered with tree roots. There was a hairy forest down there.

"I haven't seen anything like this in a while," said workman number one, while number two scratched his head and glared towards the hotel where the offending Judas tree sat innocently.

"*Oh là là!*" The words came from over my shoulder. I looked up to see Monsieur Meunier had succumbed to his curiosity and scuttled across the street to lean over my shoulder and peer into the sewer with us.

"This is not good," Sam declared. What shall we do?" he asked the water utility men.

"We'll clean out the growths," Number one informed him.

"It won't be a cure," number two said. "*Je regrette,* but they will keep growing. The real problem is the tree they come from."

Sam and I invited Alain, our neighbourhood computer expert and amateur stone mason, over for an *apéro*. He was very interested in our root problem, which had gotten around town some way or another.

"This is not good," Alain declared. "The tree roots are destabilizing this corner of your house. The wall might hold up for fifty more years or it might collapse tomorrow." He gave the Gallic shrug. "With these medieval houses, you never know. However, if the wall gives way...." He didn't need to finish his thought. It was a stout stone wall, many feet thick, but Alain showed us with his trained eye how it was starting to crack and shift under the strain of the invasive roots. If the wall did give way, the whole weighty stone house would collapse on itself.

"So, the tree has to go." Sam said. "But it isn't on our property."

"Poor me," I complained. "Besieged on both sides. Leaks from the roof of the deserted house to the left of me, *à gauche,* and now structural damage from the tree *à droite,* to my right."

"You must inform Monsieur Dieudonné," Alain said. Daniel Dieudonné was the owner of *Les Trois Terrasses* next door to us, and the owner of the tree. "Get him to remove the tree and your problems should be over."

A sensible suggestion—you'd think. However, when Sam, and I approached Monsieur Dieudonné, he was immoveable. He absolutely would not kill the tree. He stonewalled us, to make an awful pun—*un calembour.*

"What shall we do now?" I asked plaintively.

Sam had an idea. "Let's talk to Christiane, the town librarian. She grew up in Montpezat and knows everybody. You guys are friends. She likes helping us expats and showing us the ropes."

"Good idea."

And so, we invited Christiane and her husband, Camille,

the *boules* team captain, over for an *apéro* to discuss the situation. They were happy to advise us.

In their opinion, we had no choice but to find a lawyer and sue Monsieur Dieudonné in order that he cut down and destroy the offending tree. We were disappointed to be pushed into this position. It was not in our nature to litigate against our neighbors, but something had to be done.

I told Christiane, "I don't want to get involved with lawyers and lawsuits. That sounds awful. This is supposed to be my dream home," I all but wailed.

"You don't have a choice, Barbara." Christiane was pragmatic. "The tree is on his property, and you need to remove it. Even if you're willing to take full responsibility for the cost of shoring up the corner wall of your house, you must first remove the tree and its roots. And the tree is on his side of the wall; it belongs to Dieudonné.

"Anyway, my dear," Christiane went on, "*Ne t'en fais pas*, don't be upset. There are lawsuits in progress all up and down *la rue de la Libération*. These *pâtés* of houses all leaning up against one another for six hundred years or more have lots of claims and counterclaims going on. Trouble is that these lawsuits never seem to get resolved. But you can try." She gave me a smile and a wink.

"*Ouf*," I said. "I think there is a lesson here. Don't buy a medieval town house *en état*, unless you know what you are getting into – *la merde*."

Sam tried to cheer me up and pointed out all the fun we were having in Montpezat, all the nice people we had met by being summer residents in the village, the adventures made possible by living in France for part of the year.

"You're right," I was forced to concur. "I guess there's no unalloyed pleasure. You pays your ticket, you takes your chance. I'll have to think about getting a lawyer. I'll ask the *notaire* if he knows someone."

"That's the spirit,' said Sam. "We'll work it out."

I replied, "Still, if you ask me, Montpezat seems to be cursed. The houses are so old that they're at risk of falling down. Rumored artistic donations to the collégiale Saint Martin disappear without a trace. Nobody seems to ever solve any of these issues."

Sam had to agree with me. That was the 'old world' for you.

"Take a leaf out of their book, Barbara, and forget about it all for the moment. There's lots of time. Nothing happens very fast; Nothing much ever really changes, and there's not much you can do about it.

Isn't there a *marché gourmand* tonight? Let's go to the square and have a nice dinner with our friends." A *marché gourmand* was a communal dinner party under the trees on *la rue des Ecôles,* which we called Queens Boulevard because it had four lanes, two main ones in the middle and smaller ones on each side. Tonight, the street was closed to traffic and food stalls offering many delicacies were set up along the sides of enough tables and chairs for a hundred diners or more. There were several of these occasions over the summer.

"Great idea!" I enthused, catching the 'why bother' spirit. "I'll just go get a bottle of wine and my sweater." I was learning.

CHAPTER NINE
BACK IN THE USA

Sam and I bid farewell to our French friends, locked up our house, and returned to Florida for the winter. Before departing, I had found a lawyer to deal with the recalcitrant Monsieur Dieudonné and his offending tree. We were happy to consign our Montpezat problem to the back burner while we spent the winter months in Sarasota where Sam had to return to his job at the plant. We also gave up on searching for the missing Sonia Delaunay artwork. That lady seemed to finally be back in the art history books where she belonged.

Our leisure time in Sarasota was very enjoyable. Sam and I saw a lot of movies, mostly forgettable, at the Dollar Cinema. I couldn't wait to meet him after his work to catch a film. I often felt as excited as a teenager at the idea of seeing him, his face lighting up with a big smile when he spied me waiting for him by the popcorn stand.

Sitting next to each other in the darkness of the cinema or at the theater, my pulse quickened at the touch of Sam's hand in mine. Being near him, I sometimes felt a rush of languorous longing that almost made me swoon. We would sit there watching the performance and at the same time almost vibrating with passionate longing for each other.

We played golf or rather played around at playing golf. We marinated in the pool at Sam's condo and collected shells on Siesta Key beach after a storm. We ate a lot of casual and inexpensive dinners at the English Pub restaurant in the mall. We attended the winter seasons of opera and ballet for which Sarasota was well-known.

We enjoyed one another's company and companionship and our romantic attraction for one another continued to be a strong pull bonding us together.

It was silly, but fantastic, that two middle-aged, solid citizens could experience such flights of attraction for each other. Love affairs are happily possible at any age, and Sam and I were over the moon in love.

My niece Melanie had also fallen head over heels during the summer months while we were in France. She told me something about her latest boyfriend during our long-distance phone calls. I knew she had met a guy who set her heart afire and that they rode motorcycles together. Her boyfriend's name was Vernon Verdon or 'Vroom Vroom' as he was known in the motorcycling group.

The happy band of young people spent weekends riding up the west coast of Florida to the beaches around Treasure Key or down the coast to the Corkscrew Swamp.

As soon as we were back from France, Melanie came over for dinner and she and I exchanged a big hug while Sam looked on fondly. I couldn't take my eyes off her.

"Melanie," I cried. "It's great to see you! I missed you!" I studied her for a moment. "You look fine and so suntanned."

Sam, whose skin tanned very easily, laughed. "She's starting to look like a native Floridian."

"Aunt Barbara, I'm so glad you and Sam are back and that you had a great time. Yes," she said, "look at my tanned legs from riding the Harley and my arms where they stick out of my leather vest. Have you ever seen me with such tan marks?"

"And what's that tan line on your neck just below your ponytail?"

"That's from my helmet. We always wear protective gear when we ride."

"Well, that's reassuring anyway. Tell me more about this Vroom Vroom. How exciting that you have a new boyfriend and a new hobby! I must admit it all seems rather sudden and unlike you."

"Yeah, well, you'll meet Vernon soon, I've arranged for him to pick me up later, and you'll see why I'm crazy about him. Here, look at my phone. That's Vernon. What do you think?"

I studied a photo of a handsome, very suntanned young man with a charismatic smile. He sat astride a Harley Davidson motorcycle, a big hog as they said. I had to admit that he was very attractive, a bit like a young Tom Cruise.

"We'll have to have him over soon," I told Melanie. "Tell me again how you met this combination of James Dean and Steve McQueen? He looks a little dangerous."

"Actually, we met at the library. I was at the Selby Library checking out their database for my paper on Man Ray's influence on war photographer Lee Miller. The cute guy sitting next to me was humming, which bothered me, so I asked him, politely, to shut up. He was very apologetic and contrite. He explained that he couldn't get this tune out of his head from a concert he'd been to last weekend.

"I knew the concert he meant because I'd been to it, too. But I didn't tell him that. You can't really talk in a library. After an hour or so, we both were in the checkout line at the same time and Vernon introduced himself and asked me to go to the Starbucks across the street for a coffee. That's when I saw his cool leather pants.

"We left the library, and he showed me his motorcycle, which was parked near Whole Foods. We couldn't stop talking over coffee about the concert we'd seen that weekend, but I had to go. I had a class, so he offered to give me a ride back to Ringling on his bike. One thing led to another over the summer and now Vroom Vroom, isn't that a cute name, and I are a duo. I'm even thinking of getting my own motorcycle."

"Wow!" I said, dazzled by the stars in my niece's eyes. I was so pleased for her. "How does your mom feel about Vroom Vroom?" My sister, Amanda, was not the motorcycle mama type.

"Oh, you know Mom," Melanie said. "But even she can't totally object to someone like Vernon with his advanced degrees from the best universities. He's so well-educated and well-mannered. He's an accomplished nerd, who has his own start-up company. He just happens to love motorcycles and speed. You know what really impressed me that day at the library? He knew who Lee Miller was. And he knows a lot about Sonia Delaunay. Oh, that's what I want to tell you."

"Tell me what, honey?"

"Are you guys still interested in Sonia Delaunay?"

Sam and my ears perked up. After our attempts to connect the artist with Montpezat de Quercy had yielded no results, we'd thankfully shelved that topic. And then we had the wall problem arise which took all our attention. By this time our simple dinner was over, and Sam started clearing the table while we girls chatted.

"I have a gift for you guys." She retrieved a coffee table size book from the front hall and put it on the table. "Vernon and I rode up to Micanopy last weekend. Micanopy is this tiny place up north of Tampa which is a big attraction for book lovers."

"We've been there once," Sam said. "The place is as big as a minute. It's like a trip back in time. I remember the used book shops set among oak trees dripping with Spanish moss."

"That's it," confirmed Melanie. "So, Vernon and I were poking around the bookstore shelves trying to find something with a reference to Lee Miller's war photos or her connection to surrealism after the war. That's when I found a group of fashion photography books. It seems that Miller worked for Vogue magazine at one point. Anyway, Vernon was looking on the shelf next to me and he pulled out a book about Sonia Delaunay's fashion designs by Jacques Damase. The name Sonia Delaunay rang a bell, and Vernon had heard of Jacques Damase, so we bought the book and brought it home for you. Here it is."

"That is so nice of you, Melanie. You shouldn't have," I said, feeling quite touched by the gesture. Sam and I spent a few minutes looking through the beautifully illustrated volume.

"Who is Jacques Damase?" I asked.

"According to Vernon, Damase was a famous French editor and art critic in the 1960s. He was an admirer of Sonia Delaunay and went on to be her publisher and friend. She even appointed him executor of her estate when she died in 1979. Vernon says that this book is a real collector's item. Look how modern Sonia's dress designs from the 1920s are. They look like op art pieces, like Yves Saint Laurent and André Courrèges dresses from the swinging Sixties and Seventies fifty years later."

Sam and I looked at one another and the drawings, both

very impressed. "I think I see what you mean," I told Melanie, flipping slowly through the pages of colorful drawings while Sam looked over my shoulder.

"But wait," Melanie announced. "You haven't heard the best part. At the back of the fashion drawings there is a chronological listing of all of Sonia Delaunay's exhibitions and artwork *and*," she said with heavy emphasis, "written in the listing it says that Sonia Delaunay was commissioned to create a stained-glass window for the church in Montpezat de Quercy in 1966."

"Where is that notation? May I see it?" Sam asked, his attention riveted.

Melanie flipped to the listing of the artist's *catalogue raisonné* and showed us proudly the line which read *1966, stained-glass window, Montpezat de Quercy.*

"Yep. Feast your eyes. There it is in black and white."

"That is incredible! So, she designed a stained-glass window for Montpezat. That was the artwork. And now what? What shall we do with this information?" I asked wonderingly.

"Vernon and I were talking it over and we suggest that you contact the publisher, Jacques Damase, via the contact information given here on the book flap. It gives a Paris address."

"This is so exciting!" I told my wonderful, brilliant, resourceful niece. "Thank you and thanks to Vernon for his part in this discovery."

Losing no time, we all put our heads together and I composed a letter in my best French:

Cher Monsieur Damase,

My name is Barbara Waldheim. My partner, Sam

Spitz, and I are summer residents of Montpezat de Quercy. We have a house just up the hill from its church, Saint Martin. We know of and love Sonia Delaunay's artwork and are very excited at the prospect that Mme Delaunay created a stained-glass window for the collégiale, as you noted in the appendix of your beautiful book, "Sonia Delaunay, Fashion and Fabrics."

The mystery is that there is no Delaunay window in place in the collégiale. We checked. We are trying to understand what could have happened to the artwork. Can you shed any light on its disappearance? Was the window ever installed? Does it still exist?

It is our hope that you might have some information that would help us find the missing artwork and see it put in its rightful place.

Cordialement,
Barbara Waldheim

We read the missive over one last time. I intended to mail it in the morning.

"It's worth a try. How would you rate the chances we get any reply from Monsieur Damase or his agent, or whoever reads this?" I asked Sam and Melanie.

Sam said aloud what we were all thinking. "Would he still be alive after all this time?"

"Well, it's worth a try, I guess. We'll see what comes of it."

"Sure. No harm in trying," Sam chimed in.

"Goodnight, my darling," I said to Melanie as she collected her things, ready to leave. "Thank you so much for the beautiful book. I love it. Sonia's designs are like modern paintings. They could have been done yesterday."

I heard a powerful engine rounding the corner onto our street and a big motorcycle sped up the circular driveway and stopped in front of the open door.

"Hey, Aunt Barbara, I'd like you to meet Vernon Verdon."

Sam came to the doorway to see Melanie's beau. Vernon 'Vroom Vroom' Verdon was a very cordial young man. He shook our hands and greeted us as warmly as we greeted him. And no thanks, he said, he had no time to come in for a coffee but would love to another time. It was obvious he and Melanie had somewhere to be, so we let them go with promises of catching up again soon.

Melanie donned her helmet, mounted the Harley, and the two young people zoomed off into the night.

CHAPTER TEN

MONSIEUR DE GONSALVES AND MADAME DE POMPADOUR

Luck was with us, and by spring I received a response to my letter. It was an invitation, not from Jacques Damase; unfortunately, Monsieur Damase was deceased. Rather from his much younger, lifelong companion, a certain Thierry de Gonsalves, who was still living and willing to meet with us.

We'd promised Melanie a trip to France, and this seemed like the perfect opportunity. Her extensive knowledge of art history would be an asset in our interview with Monsieur de Gonsalves. There was only one fly in the ointment. At the last-minute Sam was detained at work. A rush order for hydraulic valves had come in and had to be processed before he was free to leave on vacation.

"Boy, am I ever sorry to miss out on the fun and excitement of Paris," Sam said as he dropped us off at the airport. "Call me with regular updates. Don't forget now."

"I couldn't forget you, Sam. I promise to keep touch." I said, giving him another goodbye hug over our suitcases heaped on the curb by Departures.

Melanie added brightly, "We'll meet up in Montpezat. I can't wait. We'll pick you up from Toulouse airport in ten days' time. Maybe I'll be driving the stick shift by then."

Sam's face said it all at that idea. "*I'll* be the one teaching you to drive in France," he said. "Barbara can get you started, but her shifting technique leaves a lot to be desired."

Melanie wisely let the subject go. I said nothing, thinking to myself that I always managed to get where I needed to go, even if it wasn't so pretty.

I had contacted Laure, to tell her about our visit. Like me, Laure lived elsewhere in the winter. Florida for me and Paris for her. She insisted we stay at her apartment before our rendezvous with Monsieur de Gonsalves, determined to give us a guided tour of her 'hometown' before we headed south for Montpezat and another summer. This suited Melanie down to the ground. The best way to see any foreign city was by staying with a native, *une chambre chez l'habitant*, as they say in France.

True to her word, Laure shepherded us around Paris, from the heights of Montmartre and the Moulin Rouge nightclub to the depths of the catacombs near the Eiffel Tower, with plenty of shopping in-between. One day it was the Impressionists at the Musée d'Orsay, the next the Mona Lisa at the Louvre. We shopped on the chic Faubourg St Honoré and looked for bargains at the Marché aux Puces where the flea market prices were more in keeping with our budgets. Melanie bought an old gelatin print photograph of a waterfall, which she said was a gem of a find. My niece wanted to visit Jim Morrison's grave, being a new fan of the old group The Doors. By happy coincidence, Laure's apartment was not far from the Père Lachaise cemetery where he was buried.

In the evenings, we dressed up and ventured out to explore the wonderful neighborhood bistros where the food was excellent. Once we even splashed out on a gastronomic experience at le Grand Véfour in the Palais Royal gardens.

Melanie had a great time, and I was so pleased her first experience on French soil was such a fabulous one. I just knew we had another Francophile in the family! And her French was pretty good too. My friendship with Laure deepened even further, if that was possible, at the charm and kindness she showed toward my niece. They thoroughly enjoyed each other's company, bonding over food, shopping for hip clothes, and of course, the arts. Both abounded with knowledge, and it was a pleasure to be in their company in an art gallery or museum. I learned so much! And poor Sam was jealous as I updated him every evening about our activities in the French capital.

The day of our meeting with Monsieur de Gonsalves arrived, and we were anxious to learn what he might know about the Sonia Delaunay stained-glass window intended for Montpezat's church. We stood on the steps of a little house perched high above le Parc des Buttes-Chaumont and took in its wonderful view over most of Paris.

"Wow, what a setting!" I gushed. "Imagine all the city lights at nighttime."

"Le Parc des Buttes-Chaumont isn't far from my apartment, but I never think of coming here. It's beautiful, but it doesn't have the best reputation for safety anymore," Laure said sadly.

Melanie pressed the doorbell, and we heard it reverberate inside the house. We waited for a while on the doorstep. It was very quiet and there was no one around which made me a little worried. *We haven't made a mistake, have we? This is the day and time of our appointment.*

Finally, came the scratch of a bolt being drawn on the other side of the door. It swung slowly open to reveal a frail looking, though carefully groomed gentleman, stooped with age and leaning heavily on his walking stick.

"*Excusez-moi de vous avoir fait attendre,*" he whispered in a tremulous voice. "I didn't mean to keep you waiting, but I move slowly with this cane." We were ushered into a spacious reception room furnished in vintage art deco style, the geometric decor which was all the rage in the 1940s and '50s and was now very much back in vogue. Our host bid us sit in deep leather club chairs, and on taking our seats I introduced our little group.

"*Bonjour*, thank you for seeing us, Monsieur de Gonsalves. I'm Barbara Waldheim, I sent you…, I mean Monsieur Damase, the letter concerning Sonia Delaunay. This is Madame Laure Acosta-Moneda, and my niece Melanie Renaldi."

"Ah, yes. The letter. I remember." Thierry de Gonsalves spoke slowly, the blank smile on his face making me concerned he didn't remember much at all. I waited for him to continue, but that didn't seem to be happening either. There were an uncomfortable few seconds where we all sat around looking at each other until Laure broke the silence with, "Monsieur de Gonsalves, we've come to ask you about your friend and partner, Jacques Damase.

"During his lifetime, he was very close to the artist Sonia Delaunay. We are looking for a missing artwork she created for the church in the village where we live, Montpezat de Quercy."

Monsieur de Gonsalves continued to look uncomprehending.

Laure hesitated, then rephrased the reason for our visit in

the hope of jogging his memory. "We wrote to you about our search. You invited us here today. You said you might be able to help us? You and Jacques Damase were longtime partners, and he was Sonia Delaunay's friend and manager for 16 years until she died."

A light seemed to switch on in de Gonsalves' mind. "Ah, Jacques," he said, shaking his head sadly. "And Sonia. So gifted. She received so many honors, you know. The show at the Louvre. The show at the Jeu de Paume Museum."

Melanie rode to the rescue on this sudden flash of remembrance. "Those shows were in the 1970s, weren't they, Monsieur de Gonsalves. Did you and Jacques attend them? Did you know André Malraux, he was the Minister of Culture then. He was a patron of Sonia's, wasn't he?" Her questions were angled to jog his memory, spoken in her best French.

Instead, he looked at her blankly and seemed on the verge of nodding off. My heart sank. This was a disaster. This missing artwork was jinxed.

At that moment, a handsome young man entered the room pushing a heavily laden tea cart. He was dressed in denim jeans with a tight white tee-shirt. A miniature long-haired dachshund trotted by his heels, full of self-importance. She jumped onto her owner's lap and settled in.

"*Bonjour*," the newcomer said, "I'm Jean-Charles. Tea anyone?"

"Oh, yes please," I said. I was thirsty, and the trays of cakes looked delicious. "Thank you, Jean-Charles." Laure and Melanie wasted no time following my lead.

Our host stroked the dog's silky hair as Jean-Charles poured him his tea and passed him a plate of macaroons. It seemed this was a daily routine.

The older man perked up and said in his wispy voice, "Jean-Charles helps me out around the house."

"And this adorable creature on my lap," continued Thierry de Gonsalves, seemingly refreshed by the tea, "is Madame de Pompadour, my pet 'teckel.'" I knew *teckel* meant dachshund in French. Madame de Pompadour glared at us imperiously down her long nose then she squirmed around to lick his ear with her little pink tongue as he stroked her lustrous chocolate brown coat.

As I sipped my tea and Laure made small talk in that easy Gallic way, I gazed at the dark paneled walls displaying paintings with fabulous frames and discreet illumination. They looked to be impressionist pieces, or more likely *fauves*, members of the School of Paris. *Was that red one a Vlaminck? Did I spy a Modigliani Madonna? Were these originals?* I gave Melanie a meaningful look and nodded discreetly toward the Modigliani.

She looked back at me, raising her eyebrows.

Monsieur de Gonsalves noticed our interest. *"Non, non,"* he shook his head. "The paintings are copies. *Malheureusement*, just copies. Everything has been sold." And with that, he started to weep silently.

Jean-Charles brought his employer a linen handkerchief and Madame de Pompadour licked his damp cheeks as if to comfort her master. The three of us sat there dumbstruck, feeling uncomfortable at witnessing the old man's distress.

I spoke up. "It is still a very beautiful room, Monsieur. And you have some beautiful bindings on your library bookshelves."

"Oui, Madame. La bibliothèque est encore intact. I haven't yet been forced to sell the books. The original paintings were sold off long ago to pay for upkeep and taxes. So many expenses

these days. At one time, with Jacques, money was no problem. He represented Sonia Delaunay for sixteen years. They were inseparable. Her paintings sold well. She was invited to design a sports car. She was invited to create carpets at the Royal Aubusson workshop. Françoise Hardy, a famous pop star, wore her dress designs. Dior recreated them. Everything she touched was golden..." he trailed off, exhausted by emotion. "*Excusez-moi*, I haven't been well," he said, wiping his eyes. The linen handkerchief slipped from his fingers.

Jean-Charles picked it up. "I'm sorry, *messieurs-dames*," he said. "Monsieur is upset. His *état de santé* is delicate. He hasn't been in good health for some time. I must ask you to be brief. He needs to rest."

Melanie slipped a photocopy out of her pocket and handed it to Thierry de Gonsalves who looked at it distractedly. It was the page from Jacques Damase's book listing the chronological timeline of Sonia Delaunay's artworks.

"Do you see the notation which specifies that Sonia Delaunay completed a commission for the decoration of the church of Montpezat de Quercy in 1966? We've highlighted it in yellow," she said.

De Gonsalves struggled to compose himself and consider Melanie's question. He hesitated, getting agitated again. "I don't have my glasses. It was all so long ago now. I was a very young man. My memory isn't all that it used to be," he said querulously.

Jean-Charles, who had been listening intently to the interview, anxious for it to end, walked to a display case near the bookcases and removed a small object. He put it into his employer's hand.

"Monsieur de Gonsalves," he said softly, "haven't you

always told me that this pretty little sculpture is a model of a stained-glass window Sonia designed?"

Our host held the metal *objet d'art* in his hands, he struggled slightly with its heft. The colorful little circles of glass insets gleamed gently in the black iron gridwork.

"But of course, Jean-Charles," he scolded in a firm voice, coming back to full vigor. "Haven't I always told you that this is a maquette of Sonia's church window. She got the commission from André Malraux just like Chagall did for Metz cathedral. Or like Matisse did for his chapel. She deserved it. Jacques always said she was perfect for it. Isn't that right, Madame de Pompadour?" he said, addressing his little dog who, catching her master's mood, gave throaty yips of excitement.

Our faces broke into big smiles. "May we take a photo of the model, Monsieur de Gonsalves? It would be very helpful to us," I asked. He graciously agreed and I clicked away with the camera on my iPhone.

And so, we three *mousquetaires* left the house with our booty, a photo of the model of the Delaunay stained-glass window perched next to Madame de Pompadour on her owner's lap. We left with many words of thanks, delighted that in the end, we had proof that Delaunay had been working on the Montpezat window.

The day before we were to catch the Paris train to Montpezat, where Sam would be waiting for us, Melanie wanted to visit the Musée Beaubourg. Also known as the Centre Pompidou and named for the French ex-president and lover of modern art, the architectural creation with its exoskeleton of pipes, struts, and beams, all painted in bright colors was unmissable in the chic, arty Marais quarter. We rode the exterior escalator up to the entrance to the museum. The first painting we saw on entering was, of all things, an early Sonia Delaunay.

"Isn't it wonderful, Aunt Barbara?" said Melanie. "Sonia Delaunay's art is everywhere we go in Paris. It must be a sign."

"Let's hope you're right," I replied, "and we can find her work just as easily in Montpezat de Quercy." Sonia Delaunay had come back into my life with a vengeance.

CHAPTER ELEVEN
LE MARCHÉ GOURMAND

Melanie loved Montpezat.

Sam and I had worried the little laid-back town would be too slow for her, but she fit right in, enjoying the café and bistros, our mini tours to local vineyards, old chateaus, nearby towns, and of course, St Martin's and the tapestries. She adored the medieval canons' houses behind the church that holidaymakers had turned into charming second homes. She speculated like me that the obvious place for a Delaunay window would have to be where the former stained glass had been replaced by the *grisaille* treatment. A replacement window by Delaunay wouldn't be disallowed because it would be a completely new and original work of art, grandfathered in by the approval of the Cultural Ministry.

Most evenings, if not spent with us, my niece met up with Colette, Héloïse's daughter, and headed for the Galax nightclub where the DJs spun the latest hits, *les tubes,* as they were called in French. Melanie enjoyed letting off steam with her peers after a day of sightseeing with Sam and me who were great tour guides but kind of staid.

I was glad she and Colette had hit it off. Both shared a passion for graphic novels and Manga comics, and Melanie was very encouraging of Colette's cartoon drawing classes.

On the last Saturday night of her visit, I persuaded Melanie that she should experience a rural French cultural phenomenon—the communal outdoor dinner called *le marché gourmand.* She loved the idea, so we set out down the street toward the library with our little basket holding our knives and forks. I preferred to have real silverware instead of the plastic provided by the food vendors. We brought money to buy our dinner and a few bottles of the local *Côteaux du Quercy rosé* to share with the friends we were sure to find seated at the long tables set up under the plane trees.

When we arrived at the *rue des Écoles,* we milled around the noisy, crowded street with a hundred or so other diners. The area was closed off to traffic to allow the vendor stands and trestle tables to take over. We waved greetings at seated acquaintances and kissed their cheeks, saying hello to the townspeople we knew who were in line at a food stall or clustered around the bar area. Then we spotted Laure and Pierre-Paul and sat down with them at their table.

They had just arrived from Paris that very afternoon, and Laure was delighted to meet up with Melanie again. Laure introduced us to her house guests, Blandine and Roger, her godparents, who had retired to Limoges but for many years had lived in Kenya and so spoke excellent English. Laure was very solicitous of this elderly couple, and I was pleased to spend time in conversation with them, too.

It was a busy night, diners passed by with their paper plates of food. Late arrivals checked out the main courses while the early birds had already moved on to an *éclair* or maybe an ice cream cone, *un cornet de glace,* from the dessert stands.

Young children played together on the sidewalks behind the stalls, and rock music blared here and there attracting teenagers who wanted to hang out.

At our table we opened and shared around our bottles of wine. One by one, each person or couple drifted off to buy their chosen dinner and then return to the table. Melanie, being vegan, had a limited selection but for the rest of us, there was plenty to choose from. There was sausage and *aligot,* a potato and cheese dish from the *Cantal* region to the north of the *Tarn-et-Garonne.* The *aligot* was pulled like taffy until its ingredients, mashed potatoes and *Cantal* cheese, were entirely amalgamated. The *aligot* went well with the grilled sausage. This was Sam's favorite.

I liked it, too, but usually chose duck. There were several duck selections available, this being the southwest of France. You could have *salade quercynoise,* with thin slivers of smoked duck wings and a slice of duck *foie gras.* The big salad also included walnuts and goat cheese as well as *gésiers,* duck gizzards cooked to a velvety smooth consistency. There was also *le magret,* duck breast, the choicest part of the bird, served rare with *pommes soufflées,* very thinly sliced fried potatoes which puffed up when cooked in duck fat. Or I might choose duck *confit,* the duck leg and thigh preserved in duck fat—a cholesterol feast slightly mitigated by its accompaniment, a green salad.

Alain appeared beside me with his girlfriend Françoise, and they squeezed into our table. He had selected a healthy bowlful of shiny mussels, *moules marinières,* simply prepared sailor style, cooked in a broth of white wine with butter and onion, while Françoise chose a *crêpe* from Brittany. It looked so delicious I almost changed my mind on the duck. A thin layer of *crêpe* batter was poured onto a big, round griddle to cook. It was flipped over and filled with seafood or cheese and folded into a floppy, flat package which was brown and crispy at the edges.

Alain's friends, Jojo and Chloé, oversaw the *crêperie* stall. Jojo, short for Georges, had owned a restaurant on the *Côte d'Azur* before retiring to Montpezat. He cooked and served with a flourish. He was a handsome man, and his wife Chloé was a delicate blonde. They prepared a special ratatouille crepe for Melanie that met her dietary requirements and was so delicious she declared she was in heaven. Jojo was very pleased by her praise.

There was something lovely in the casual, relaxed atmosphere of the street dinner party and its idyllic setting under the rows of trees lining the *rue des Écoles* that put people at ease with one another. As the evening wore on, I could see that Melanie was appreciating the special charm of the gathering. Her French was serviceable but lots of the guests spoke some English and people were interested to talk with her.

"Is it always like this, Aunt Barbara?" she asked, her eyes sparkling in the lights trailing from the trees overhead. "This is wonderful."

"Usually, but tonight is special because it's the beginning of summer and everyone is here," I answered honestly. "Sometimes it's just Sam and me and we share a table with folks we don't know. We've met some nice people like that. Some are tourists from different parts of France touring the Tarn-et-Garonne region."

"So," Pierre-Paul said, "Laure has been telling me about your visit to Thierry de Gonsalves."

"It was very successful," I said.

Laure agreed. "Now we have actual photographic proof."

"What will you do next?" Melanie asked.

"Gosh." I turned to Laure. "What *do* we do next?"

"I suggest you bundle up your evidence and go over the heads of the local "experts" to the Ministry of Culture," Pierre-Paul said.

Sam agreed with him. "That's a great idea. How can we do that? We need to go straight to the top."

He was right, of course. If we could get the attention of the present Minister of Cultural Affairs who was one of the most prominent women in the government, we might get some action. It might not be a simple matter to put our case before her given the layers of French bureaucracy, but once we did, she would probably be as excited about a woman artist's lost masterpiece as we were.

Laure and I exchanged glances and raised our glasses to each other, *Santé*. Together, we were up to the task if we could just figure out how to proceed.

"You know," I said, a thought occurring to me. "We need to get this information we discovered in Paris officially documented the way I did for my tree problem with my neighbor. That way we will have a persuasive case compiled by an objective third party to present to Madame Minister."

"You mean hire a *huissier de justice* to retrace our steps and take photographs and interview de Gonsalves and his aide about our visit? That could be costly," Sam pointed out.

Pierre-Paul was undeterred. "But that would be a way to get the minister's attention. Our claims would be taken seriously. And if we all share the cost, it won't hurt too much."

"The report and accompanying photos that my *huissier* from Caussade put together helped me to get a good result about the tree and my crumbling wall. Do you know any *huissiers de justice* in Paris?"

Laure spoke up. "My brother is a notary in Paris. He will know the name of a *huissier* we can contact."

"There you go! You've got it!" Melanie exclaimed. "You guys make a good team, and you're good tour guides, too. I really enjoyed my visit with you. Thank you for all the fascinating things we did and sights we saw. I'll miss you, all of you. Good luck on your mission."

CHAPTER TWELVE
WONDERFUL THINGS!

Sam and I felt a bit flat after Melanie left. Her youthful energy had added a zing to our lives, as it always did. But we were soon absorbed by the drama of the Judas tree and Monsieur Dieudonné.

While we were away over the winter, the long arm of the law had compelled Daniel Dieudonné to remove the Judas tree from his courtyard. Moreover, his insurance company had agreed to pay to rebuild our endangered wall, which was fantastic news for us.

The premier masons of Montpezat, *les frères* Théron, the two Théron brothers, had agreed to do the restoration. Another wonderful development. People usually had to wait a very long time for the Thérons' expert services, so Sam and I felt very fortunate they'd taken on the job—honored even.

Achille Théron, father and head of the family business, stopped by to survey the problem for himself. As we stood on the sidewalk in front of my house, he said that, in his opinion, this job was very urgent, and he wanted to begin as soon as possible. And so, his sons appeared the next week and got down to work.

I found out a little later that Monsieur Théron, *père*, was also mayor of nearby Montfermier, a little hamlet just across the *route nationale* from Montpezat. He felt he had a civic duty to make sure that houses didn't go collapsing in his backyard, and especially not around the ears of a couple of nice Americans!

When he was in the French army, he had loved shopping in the US Army post exchange, the PX, to which all the troops had access. He fondly remembered the PX's cornucopia of goodies at low prices and so he was very well-disposed toward Americans.

As promised, his sons started working almost immediately, first by installing an enormous framework of scaffolding. It had to hold the entire weight of our four-story stone house while they tore down, and then rebuilt our wall. Several tons of stone had to be supported by these braces or *étais* while they worked. It seemed a risky business to us although it was all in a day's work for the Thérons.

A new cornerstone was to be dressed and laid in place. The beautiful, creamy limestone block duly arrived in a truck and had to be craned carefully in place. Alain, our apprentice stonemason neighbor, was a frequent visitor to the worksite, *le chantier*.

The work was taking place right inside our entryway, making it hard to lock up the house securely as there was a big hole where the front door should be. The Thérons did the best they could to jerry rig a door, of sorts, and luckily for us, we lived in a very safe place.

Passersby surveyed the progress of the work as it progressed. Some were very curious and others hardly gave the scaffolding a cursory glance. Monsieur Meunier, from across the street, often came over to put in his two cents since he was a self-appointed expert in every domain. The Thérons kindly put up with him for the most part.

The following Friday as Sam and I returned from market day in Caussade laden with our weekly grocery shopping, we saw Michel Théron signaling us to come over.

"*Venez voir.* We have something to show you."

"We'll be right there," I said. "Just let us put our *provisions* away." We put the meat, fish, and cheeses in our little refrigerator and left the paper bags of fruit and vegetables on the marble counter and went to find Michel. He was behind the plastic sheeting which shielded our living space from the work area.

Arnauld came down from the scaffolding to join us. He was the older brother and usually did the talking. "There's a basement under this house. *Quelle surprise!* My brother and I were digging the foundation for the new wall, and we uncovered this entrance to a *cave* or *sous-sol* under the floor in this little alcove. Did you know about it?"

"No!" Sam and I said in unison. We looked at one another. We had always thought there was a funny aura about this little area. We peered down into the deep, dark hole with cobwebbed steps yawning open in our floor.

"What shall we do about it?" Arnauld asked. "We can cover it back up."

Michel nodded. "*C'est le plus simple.* That would be the easiest."

"Hm, what do you think, Barbara? Should they just close it up?" Sam asked.

"Maybe we should investigate a little before we seal it off again. Who knows what we'll find? A treasure?" I winked at the men. "I just know there's something special about this alcove space."

"*D'accord*," Arnould agreed. "We're going to knock off for the weekend anyway, so you have some time to think it over."

"*Au revoir, passez un bon weekend.*" I waved the Thérons off down the *rue de la Libération* in their dusty, white truck.

Sam and I didn't waste a moment. He went first down the narrow stone staircase using the flashlight on his cell phone to guide us, and I followed. At the bottom, we found ourselves in a low-ceilinged chamber. Although neither one of us was particularly tall, we had to stoop in the cramped space.

Sam scoped out the corners with the weak light from his phone. It was a strange feeling to be underneath our house where we ate meals, received guests, relaxed, and generally went about our daily lives.

"We need a real flashlight," I said, not liking the creepy darkness one bit. "I can't see much with the light from your phone. We could trip down here."

"Do we have a flashlight?" Sam asked me, over his shoulder.

"I'm not sure."

"Let's get out of here and I'll go ask Laure and Pierre-Paul if they have one. How do you say flashlight in French?"

"*Lampe de poche,*" I informed him.

"Okay, I'll only be a minute. I can't wait to show Pierre-Paul what the masons found. From the little I can see, it looks like it would make a great wine cellar."

Sam was back right away with Pierre-Paul carrying *une lampe de poche* in his hand. Laure was out for the day with her godparents, Blandine and Roger. I knew she'd be disappointed at missing the action, but she'd see our latest *découverte* when she returned home. Sam moved aside the plastic sheeting and showed the stone stairs to Pierre-Paul.

"*O la vache*, what is this place?" His eyes widened.

Once more we descended into the dark. The flashlight's beam bounced off the roughly hewn stone walls. The floor was tamped earth and uneven to walk on. We placed our feet carefully so as not to fall.

"*C'est incroyable!* Who would have expected this hidden chamber? These houses from the Middle Ages can be full of surprises." Pierre-Paul was a six-footer and bent almost double. "*Attention à la tête, mes amis!* Let's not bump our heads on the low ceiling."

Sam said, looking around, "What do you think, Pierre-Paul? This would make a great wine cellar, *n'est-ce pas?*"

"*Et comment!* You could safely store quite a few bottles down here. I'm sure the temperature remains a constant 13 *degrés celsius* all year round. Perfect for wine preservation."

"Is it getting cooler?" I noticed how chilly the air was. "I'm glad I'm wearing a long-sleeved tee-shirt. Are you guys warm enough?" They sported tees, shorts and sandals.

The guys were occupied. Sam was studying the wall to the left, no doubt planning where to put the wine racks. Pierre-Paul went toward the farthest end of the cavity. Suddenly, he gave a yelp and almost lost his balance.

"*Ça alors!* What have we here? *Venez vite!* There are more steps! There seems to be a further passageway." Pierre-Paul's flashlight picked out a low archway at the far side of the cellar. We could barely see a few feet beyond, but it seemed as if the opening led on into the interminable darkness.

Although it was foolhardy, as we would recount to Frederic Bruneau of *les Monuments Historiques de France* in his office in Montauban on Monday, we couldn't resist exploring further. Cautiously, we advanced through the archway and found ourselves in a narrow but well-constructed tunnel that was in remarkably good condition. This passage was much roomier than the chamber under our house so that eventually even Pierre-Paul could walk upright. It led us onward on a decline, and we could sense the steepness of the slope under our feet. We walked along it for about ten minutes guided by the light from the flashlight until the tunnel came to a halt. Our way forward was blocked by a tumble of stones and several old wooden crates piled haphazardly on top of each other.

Peering through gaps in the collapsed stone, we could hardly believe our eyes. Beyond, we made out the crypt of the *collégiale*. Sam and I immediately recognized it from our last visit there with Frédéric.

"Is that..." Sam was momentarily at a loss for words.

"It is. I think it is!" I cried.

"What? What is it?" Pierre-Paul was not aware of what we were looking at. He had never seen the crypt.

"Pierre-Paul," I explained, "We've literally traveled underground down the hill from our house to Saint Martin's! We've discovered one of the ancient tunnels that leads to *la collégiale*."

"*Sans blague. Un souterrain,*" Pierre-Paul said in a stage whisper. We felt as if we had trespassed into the underworld. We all shivered in the cool air, thoroughly excited but wary.

"I can't believe it. We've discovered one of the medieval tunnels that Frédéric Bruneau speculated might exist," Sam said. We looked at one another in astonishment. Could this really be happening?

"What are these crates?" Pierre-Paul wondered aloud, flashing the light on the wooden boxes clustered around the collapsed stone. "Shall we peek inside?"

"Maybe it's part of the archaeological equipment stored

here by the *Monuments Historiques*," I suggested. "Frédéric said they kept equipment in the crypt."

"Ah," Pierre-Paul said sagely. "Then we mustn't touch, right?"

Nobody said anything for a few beats. Pierre-Paul cast his flashlight over the packing boxes. They were very dirty, covered with thick layers of dust and cobwebs and looked as if they had been undisturbed for decades. He rubbed at the dusty lettering on the nearest crate. I bent for a better look and made out the initials *SD*, written in red inside a yellow circle.

"That's odd," I said. "The label doesn't look like anything to do with *les Monuments Historiques de France,* does it?" voicing our growing suspicions.

"Well, if it's not Frederic's scientific stuff maybe we can look inside?" Sam said.

"Maybe there's a body," Pierre-Paul half-joked. "You said we're near the crypt."

"Oh, don't say that Pierre-Paul. You're creeping me out." I shivered a little with cold and excitement.

Sam took a pen knife out of his pocket and worked away at a corner of a box. The lid gave way slowly until he and Pierre-Paul could pry it a little looser with their fingers. I squatted down to peer inside. There was a layer of straw which I carefully pushed aside.

I gasped.

"What? What do you see?"

"Can you see anything?" Pierre-Paul and Sam spoke over each other.

I felt like Howard Carter unsealing King Tut's tomb for the first time.

"What do you see?" Sam asked again.

And I answered just as Carter did in Egypt all those years ago, "Wonderful things!"

I was looking at dozens of colored glass pieces protected by the straw packing. The multi-colored glass sparkled like jewels in the beam of the flashlight. The fragments I could make out were varied in size. Some were smooth, some had raised relief.

"Oh, my God," I said. Moving aside to give Sam and Pierre-Paul room to look for themselves. "The initials *SD* must stand for Sonia Delaunay. Have we just found the missing stained-glass window?"

CHAPTER THIRTEEN

PURSUING WONDERFUL THINGS

The scientist in Frédéric Bruneau put an unexpected dampener on our discovery. He was more interested in the discovery of the tunnel than the crates of glass and a possible coup for the art world!

We met up with him at his office at *les Monuments Historiques de France* where our excitement was soon restrained by his talk about empirical evidence and associated documentation. We'd found a tunnel, that much was undeniable and all that really interested him was that it proved his theory that Montpezat was riddled with underground tunnels. Now he wanted to examine every inch of it and seemingly take a long time doing so, while locking down the tunnel until he'd finished. It could take years! *And* nothing was to be moved or touched until then, including the crates.

"This is potentially explosive," he said. "The authorities will be compelled to fund me. It will expand the scope of my research exponentially. As soon as I have the extra equipment, my team and I will go onsite. Of course, *we* won't be taking the risks you did. Safety will be the priority. You three were lucky to walk away in one piece. Frankly, I'm worried there may be some damage with you all barreling in there like Rambo."

"Rambo!" I exploded. "You should be thanking us. And what about the crates? If they contain the missing Delaunay window they need to be removed before any harm comes to them. They're much more important."

Frederic bridled at that. "Nothing is to be touched until we have secured the tunnel and done an initial survey," he said. He was unmoveable on this.

"And how long will that take?" Sam asked, much more calmly than me. He got an eloquent shrug in reply.

"First, I need to do the paperwork. It takes time. Someone from the Ministry may well visit in the meantime to make an initial assessment—"

"That will take ages," Pierre-Paul objected. "Why should your project take priority over ours? We made the discovery after all. We're only asking for the question of the crates to be resolved first. It's obvious they are not archaeological and of no interest to *les Monuments Historiques*."

Good for him! I was glad he was just as adamant as I was. Go, Pierre-Paul! *Allez!*

Frédéric stood up from his desk and spread his hands in a placating manner. "You have my sympathy, but things must be done in the correct manner. I am the official and my project takes priority every time. *Your* project is apparently an assortment of glass pieces you have somehow imagined into a full-blown, stained-glass window with nothing to go on."

"But we won't know until we get the crates out and examine the contents," I cried. "And we *do* have something to go on. We have photographic evidence from a contemporary of Sonia Delaunay as to what she was commissioned to make.

We'll know what we're looking at *if* we can get a chance to look at it."

"Evidence?" Frederic frowned. "This is news to me."

"We've already sent an official report compiled in *bonne et due forme* to the Ministry of Cultural Affairs," Pierre-Paul told him. "We arranged for a *huissier de justice* to document our case and her report, *le constat,* has been submitted to Madame Minister. It certifies that our visit to Thierry de Gonsalves, Jacques Damase's companion, took place and that we took a photo of the Sonia Delaunay maquette, which Gonsalves assured us was a model of the stained-glass window designed for the collégiale. Yours is not the only office involved in this affair."

"*Aha*" Frederic seemed to mull this over, impressed by this development. "I didn't know that you had taken this step."

A *huissier de justice* was an officer of the French courts who could be called as an objective third party witness. The report we had asked our *huissier* to put together guaranteed the veracity of our claims and laid out the evidence.

Alright then, Frédéric said in conclusion, "I will check into this and follow the correct protocols." And with that, the interview was over.

———

Pierre-Paul's words about the Ministry of Cultural Affairs' involvement in the matter were effective. To my surprise and pleasure, a team of researchers arrived at our house the next morning, but not archaeologists, they were art conservationists from Paris come to carefully remove the crates.

"I think Frédéric's realized it's best to get the glass out of the way so he can get on with his own work," Sam said. "It's probably occurred to him that *les Monuments Historiques* will have to play second fiddle to the Ministry of Cultural Affairs, especially where an important lost work of art from a world-renowned artist is involved."

Poor Frédéric, our little crate conundrum had to be dealt with first before work on his tunnels could begin properly. He turned up along with the conservation team in a convoy of several cars and a government van. There were several conservators, dressed in white coveralls with respirators. They quickly disappeared down the opening to the cellar below. It looked like a newly discovered murder scene, and I was vaguely aware of curtains twitching in the windows of the houses opposite ours, especially from Claude Meunier's house.

Frédéric was also suited and booted. He was here in his official capacity. This was his turf, and he particularly wished to oversee the delicate removal of the crates and ensure no harm was done to his tunnel. In archaeological terms, the tunnel was a protected environment. And so, our house was once again taken over by strangers coming and going and raising plumes of dirt and dust. It was a good thing that I liked to vacuum!

"What do they plan to do with the crates of glass, Frédéric?" I asked. I was very possessive of those crates.

"They will be carefully transported to Montauban. It's too big a risk to take them as far as the Ministry of Cultural Affairs' headquarters in Paris, so they have taken over part of my offices in the meantime."

"Oh," I said a little snarkily. "They must be important then."

"Mostly because they are filled with glass," Frederic said rather defensively, and for a moment I saw Monsieur Bruneau the Senior shining through the son. "It's too delicate for much movement."

"And then what will they do?"

Frédéric stood more erect. "Although this is not my usual area, I am the senior official in charge, at least for now. My team will try and form a cohesive ensemble using the photographic evidence you have already supplied to the Ministry."

"Oh," I said. "Like a jigsaw puzzle kind of thing."

"Exactly like a jigsaw...kind of thing," he conceded, and relaxed a little. At least he was in charge, even if he didn't care too much for this aspect of the work and was itching to get on with investigating the tunnel.

"Well, that's great for you." I tried my diplomacy skills. "If it is the Delaunay this could be big."

We stood aside as a crate was lifted from our new cellar by many careful hands and carted out the non-existent door.

"Then you can get on with the important work of mapping out the tunnel," Sam added, picking up on the trend of the conversation.

"In time, yes." Frederic was still miffed the crates were of more importance, at least for the moment.

"Hopefully, a lot more funding will come to Saint Martin's," Sam continued, accentuating the positive. "I mean, a tunnel and a missing artwork, that's two big discoveries in one."

Frederic grudgingly smiled at the thought of his future laurels. "*If* it is the missing artwork."

"May we watch them assemble the glass, Frédéric?" I inquired. "Maybe we can be of help?"

The answer was negative. "Barbara, I understand that you are very invested in the outcome, but the best thing you and Sam can do for the time being is stay out of the way of the experts." And he turned on his heel and followed the last crate out the door.

———

In the meantime, news of a dead body in our cellar had traveled around the village with the speed of light. We tried our best, along with Laure and Pierre-Paul, to correct the stories whenever we could but tongues were wagging.

Nothing put these crazy rumors to rest until Jacques Bro, reporter for *La Dépêche,* our town's newspaper, wrote an article telling what had really been discovered underneath our house. The truth hit the village and the surrounding villages of *La Dépêché's* circulation area, hot off the press. Quiet little Montpezat reeled from the news that a newly discovered ancient tunnel—interesting for sure—was hiding a possible long-lost work of art by a famous modern artist.

A full-page spread appeared featuring an article on our discoveries and a picture of us, Sam, Pierre-Paul, Laure and I all in a row with head researcher-in-charge, Monsieur Frédéric Bruneau in the middle holding a photo of the Delaunay glass window maquette in front of his chest like a *boules* tournament trophy.

The article carefully pointed out that it was not yet proven that the glass pieces were from a Delaunay, but this caveat was mostly overlooked by the readership.

This article was followed shortly by another piece in *La Dépêche.* The Hébrard family, who owned a farm towards *La Madeleine,* a commune of Montpezat de Quercy, came forward with a letter that Madame Delaunay had written to their great-grandmother, Pascale Hébrard in 1944.

The newspaper printed it in its entirety. It was a sort of

thank you note to the Hébrard family for their offer to shelter Sonia at their farm—an invitation which had never been taken up since the war ended in time. The last sentences of the missive said:

Some way, somehow, if and when I am able in the future, I will repay your generosity and bravery. If you are an example of the kind of people who live in Montpezat de Quercy, I commend your greatness of spirit and I will never forget you.

Sincerely,
Sonia Delaunay

After these articles appeared, Frédéric, Pierre-Paul, Laure, Sam and I became celebrities. People strolled by our house, trying to sneak a peek at the tunnel entrance.

Frédéric complained, "We shouldn't have broken this news prematurely. This place is now a circus."

Frédéric did have a point, but he also seemed content to bury Sonia all over again, and that didn't seem fair either.

Finally, he had the area sealed off from public view, which left Sam and me with limited access to our own house. The mess was tedious and getting us down, but before we could get too upset about it, we got a very generous offer from our neighbor, Daniel Dieudonné. The man who had owned the Judas tree.

Despite past frictions, Daniel now wanted to help and offered to put us up in his beautiful *chambre d'hôtes* until the excavation work could be sealed off from our living space. We happily accepted his gracious offer of hospitality. As Sam told him, "Daniel, you're a godsend." This was a little bit of a joke because his last name, *Dieudonné,* meant "sent by God" in French.

"Why do you think he's doing this?" Sam asked, as we unpacked our things in our new sumptuous bedroom. "Not that I'm complaining. It's a very fine gesture."

"I suppose, in a way he sees his tree and its demise as somehow part of this wonderful discovery," I mused, putting my clothes away in *l'armoire.* "And maybe it makes him feel he's part of it all, too."

"The whole town wants to be part of it," Sam answered, which was true.

As we went about our business in the village, people stopped to congratulate us.

Claude Meunier was so proud of his position as our immediate neighbor that we thought he might burst. We ran into *Monsieur le Maire,* who shook Sam's hand mightily and gave me *la bise* on both cheeks and one more for good measure.

Even in Caussade, the biggest town near to Montpezat, we were surprised to find that many people knew who we were and gave us friendly nods and knowing smiles in the street as we ran our everyday errands. It was a lot of fun, and along with Laure and Pierre-Paul we were enjoying the attention. However, in the back of our minds, we were on tenterhooks to learn the verdict of the art conservationists and historians who had been brought in to examine the contents of the crates. Had we uncovered the Sonia Delaunay window or not?

Frédéric was our only point of contact, and he was hard to pin down. His reports were cautious. "The style and composition of the glass while being consistent with the late 1960s, and supposedly in line with Delaunay's shapes and color palette, is not wholly acceptable as proof of anything. The crates and the monograms printed on them mean nothing and can't be used as an attribution to the artist," he droned on.

He was a real killjoy of the highest order.

"The problem," he opined, "is that with only the little maquette as a guide," Frédéric had Thierry de Gonsalves' original maquette on loan by now, "assembling a full-scale church window is a jigsaw puzzle without a jigsaw puzzle lid to follow the design. The maquette is just too little for the detail needed. It was only meant to be a display item after all. A toy."

We were perplexed. We were indignant. He was stalling over the tiniest details. But it made sense.

"Without relevant paperwork, there is really no connection between these crates full of colorful glass, undated, unindexed, no provenance of any kind, and a stained-glass window for Saint Martin's," he concluded.

"Remember when his father postulated his private opinion that modern art had no place in a medieval context. Could Frédéric be of the same opinion?" Laure asked.

We had fifty arguments as to why and how Frédéric should overcome his hesitations. We were having an *apéro* at Laure and Pierre-Pauls's place. Drowning our perplexity and sorrows in an early evening cocktail.

"The problem is the lack of paperwork. There must be some somewhere," Laure declared. "I cannot believe the Minister of Culture commissioned this piece and not one bit of evidence exists."

"Who would have been in charge in the Sixties," Pierre-Paul asked.

"André Malraux," I answered.

"Not him, I mean here, in Montpezat."

"Um," Laure looked thoughtful. Out of all of us she was the only one who could answer that question. Her family had a home here for generations. "Why, Bruneau. Frédéric's father. At least I think so."

"You don't think he's buried the paperwork through some personal grudge against modern art?" I asked.

"I can't see it. He's too civic minded," Laure replied with a signature shrug.

Sam had been sitting quietly listening to the rest of us. "You know, I've been doing some math in my head. I calculate that Frédéric's dad would have been too young in the 1960s to have been in charge of the church. If Saint Martin's has always been a Bruneau family affair, more likely it was Fred's grandfather who was the collégiale expert and protector at that time."

"Ohhhh," the rest of us let out a collective gasp of air as the logic of this realization set in. How could we not have seen that, I wondered. I had heard it somewhere before, but now it made sense.

"But does that really matter," Pierre-Paul spoke up. "We're still missing the vital documentation that would show how to assemble the glass into a full-fledged window and which space in the church it was designed for.

Laure's telephone rang and she answered. She motioned to us with her hand that we should keep quiet for a minute. When she hung up, she told us, "You'll never guess who that was?" Expectant silence. "It was Frédéric, and we're all invited over to his father's house next to the collégiale tomorrow evening for an apéro. He has some big news for us."

———

We four *mousquetaires* trudged down the hill to *chez Bruneau* the following evening cautiously optimistic that the logjam had broken. As we got settled on the Bruneau's terrace with a bottle of wine and an assortment of *crudités*, Monsieur Bruneau Senior spent some time on pleasantries. We complimented him on the beautiful valley views from his house, and the excellence of the wine he had chosen for tonight's visit, a new blend created by the Côteaux de Quercy wine cooperative. I could see Laure, along with myself, was becoming restless as to why we were there. Eventually, Monsieur Bruneau got to the point.

"Frédéric arrived here the other evening with a very interesting *idée*," he began. "That we should investigate my own father, Guy Bruneau's, papers. He was, after all, the caretaker of the *collégiale* before me."

Sam dropped me a wink. "Aha," he seemed to say.

"The Bruneau family has always viewed our responsibility for the *collégiale* as a sacred trust, to be exercised with the utmost care and probity," Bruneau solemnly lectured us.

He cleared his throat, and his next words were, "*Messieurs-dames*, you will never believe what just turned up in my library. I have discovered the detailed drawings and plans for the Sonia Delaunay window hidden between the pages of one of my father's books. It seems that my father, guide and protector of the *collégiale* before my time, somehow misplaced or lost these documents back in the 1960s during his tenure."

There were many murmurs of disbelief. Firstly, at such a catastrophic oversight, and secondly that despite all the odds the original paperwork had been unearthed at all.

Sensing the mood, Frédéric jumped to his father's defence. "We are, of course, profoundly embarrassed. It should never have occurred had my grandfather's papers been properly archived."

"I should say so! How could such significant papers have been tucked in between the pages of a book?" Laure was not letting the Bruneau's off so easily.

Frédéric's cheeks reddened, and he hurried on. "There can no longer be any doubt as to the artist's identity or any impediment to the reconstruction of her artwork with these papers as a guideline." He grabbed his wine goblet and raised it high. "*Mes amis,*" he cried, "I salute you and all your efforts. Let's toast to the latest jewel soon to adorn our *collégiale, un vitrail signé Sonia Delaunay,* a Sonia Delaunay stained-glass window!"

Champagne appeared as if by magic or brought in on a tray by Madame Bruneau. We toasted each other and all tension quickly dissipated. This was a magnificent development for Saint Martin's, and despite Bruneau Senior's *faux-pas,* his beloved church would benefit greatly from it.

Niggling questions crowded my mind, and perhaps always would. Had Monsieur Guy Bruneau really mislaid such important documentation? Had he stonewalled the installation of a work of modern art in the medieval church? Had he especially opposed an avant-garde woman artist's creation in his church? Had he taken advantage of the change in the political winds in the late 1960s when Minister of Culture André Malraux had lost his position to brazenly scuttle the commission? And who had hidden the boxes in the crypt? The people with these answers I suspected were no longer with us.

In a magnanimous gesture, local heiress and art collector, Laure Acosta-Moneda offered to help subsidize the assembly and installation of the new window into Saint Martin's. A stupendously generous offer from a true patron of the arts.

I raised my champagne flute along with everyone else and exalted that despite the odds, Sonia's art piece would eventually see the light of day.

CHAPTER FOURTEEN

A STAINED-GLASS WINDOW SIGNÉ DELAUNAY

One morning, happily ensconced at the Trois Terrasses, Sam and I were enjoying the lovely breakfast Daniel Dieudonné provided for his *chambre d'hôtes* guests each day. When our host sat down to join us at the table, we thanked him again for his hospitality. He said impatiently, "*Ça suffit.* You have thanked me enough. I want to tell you what I heard in town at the bakery this morning. Did you know that Héloïse Dutoit, the woman who precipitously inherited the former mayor's house after his ill-timed demise, wants to help finance the cost of mounting and installing the Delaunay window? Isn't that nice? I heartily approve of her gesture."

I thought to myself here was another person in the village taking this opportunity to rehabilitate their image. Good for her! Since the French cultural authorities were perennially short of funds, the more people involved in supporting the expense of getting the window in place, the sooner it would happen.

"That is wonderful news, isn't it Sam," I said to my partner who was already brushing the crumbs of his croissant off his lap and preparing to stand up. "Yes, it's super. The more the merrier. But you know, Daniel, Frédéric is giving us a tour of the glass workshop this morning. We should get going if we don't want to be late."

We said goodbye to Daniel and set off down the hill to the temporary structure the village municipal workers had built to house the artisans involved in the project. Frédéric Bruneau had offered to give us a glimpse into the area where the art restorers were hard at work fitting together the glass sections of the window carefully following Madame Delaunay's drawings and written instructions found in the Bruneau's library.

He was there to greet us as arranged, and we said *bonjour* and exchanged *bises*. The *atelier* was a beehive of activity in technicolor. There were hundreds of pieces of colored glass of all shapes, sizes and thicknesses spread out on tables shining in the light. The researcher picked up a yellow glass section to show us. It glinted merrily. "See how the artist has painted in black on this piece to give it dimension? We leaned in for a closer look.

"According to her notes, Madame Delaunay used slight variations in treatment of the glass depending on the final effect she wanted to achieve, calculating how the finished window would appear in its final form reacting to the light. The glass pieces themselves are works of the glass maker's art. Look at the gradations of color and intensity and the quality of the material." We admired other pieces of glass which Frédéric held up for our examination.

"How does it all get put together, Fred," I asked, fascinated. "Will it be heavy?

"It works like this," he told us. "It is hard to estimate the weight for finished stained-glass panels. Aside from the overall size of a panel, another factor is the lead which holds the glass together. The lead comes in many sizes. The various lead widths which Madame Delaunay specified for different sections of the window add another expressive element to the design. These lead pieces are called *came.* This word has nothing to do with the slang word *la came* which you might know."

We all laughed because *la came* in modern French slang means hard drugs like cocaine and heroin. Frédéric picked up his explanation of the stained-glass *came.* "They come in two kinds," he said. "There are the H shaped sections which hold two pieces together and the U-shaped sections used for the borders." We peered at the examples he pointed out.

"These *came* or divider bars are used between small pieces of glass to make a larger glazing panel and hold the glass together. They are applied at the final stage. *Came* are made of lead, zinc, copper, or brass. Of the metals, lead is softer and more flexible, making it easier to cut and bend. The harder metals are used to work with slightly curved lines and pieces that require greater structural support. They can also be used as borders, once again for stability and support. This part of the process also demands a certain artistry."

He continued, "a section of glass is laid out according to Madame Delaunay's pattern and soldered together with *came.* The sections are mounted in frames which must fit the window opening, in this case the window in the side chapel. Then the leaded frames are mounted in place in stages for a big window like this one. Madame Delaunay designed her window to fit in the baroque side chapel just inside the main door, the one where the stained-glass window was replaced.

Well, that made sense. It's just what Melanie and I had foreseen. I asked to be sure, "You mean the chapel where the alabaster sculptures are now? The ones in the cases, the *vitrines,* which show Christ ascending to heaven? Will they stay there under Sonia's window?"

"That's the side chapel I mean," Fred said. "And I don't see why the little sculptures wouldn't stay there."

"Thank you for allowing us this visit," Sam told Frédéric. "We'll leave you to get on with your work. I can see it's a big project."

"Yes, it is a big project that will take time to bring to fruition. But we want it to be perfect, right? And to last for posterity." Our heads bobbed up and down in agreement.

Despite past missteps or controversies, the important collective goal was now to see the Delaunay window mounted in the side chapel of the *collégiale* for which it had been intended, the damaged one. It was as if her window was putting things right.

We walked back up the hill to our accommodation at the Trois Terrasses, both of us reflecting on what we had seen and learned. "What an enormous project, *un travail de titan,*" I commented to Sam, "Frédéric seems to have everything well in hand though. I was impressed.

"I'm so pleased that the *grisaille* window will be replaced. I always felt it detracted from the whole effect," I insisted. "And what a glorious replacement! I can't wait to see what Sonia Delaunay planned for that space. I wonder how she will make it fit in."

Sam responded with his usual good sense, "Maybe instead of trying to blend in, her design is so different in feeling that it will work by contrasting."

"That's an interesting thought. I guess we'll just have to wait and see. We won't be seeing the new window installed anytime soon," I contributed.

Work proceeded on assembling the glass window. We *mousquetaires* from Montpezat were very much on the sidelines. Our daily lives were just calming down to a dull roar when the national media got hold of our story and we were the center of attention once again—our fifteen minutes of fame, as Andy Warhol named the phenomenon.

It all started the evening that the segment about us was broadcast on TV. All three French television channels showed coverage of the tunnel and the stained-glass window and the role we had played in finding them.

I got a telephone call from my friend, Micheline Dubosc, in Paris. "Barbara!" she said breathlessly. "I can't believe it! You didn't tell me! You and Sam are heroes. I just saw you on the *Canal Un* news with the most famous news presenter of all! You looked wonderful. *Félicitations!* It turns out your medieval townhouse was a good purchase after all. I always said there was something I liked about it. Put Sam on the line. I want to congratulate him, too."

Sam picked up the phone receiver. "Bonjour Michou." Sam called Micheline by her nickname. "How's my girl?"

"Sam, I saw you on TV with Barbara and the others. The reporter also interviewed that old man who owns a *maquette* of the stained-glass window."

"Monsieur de Gonsalves is his name," Sam prompted her.

"Yes, he and his dog, they were so endearing," Micheline went on. "Monsieur de Gonsalves was quite obviously moved to be a part of the excitement. He had tears in his eyes. It was touching, *touchant, vraiment touchant.* He reminded me of my dear departed husband, Paul. You don't remember Paul. He died before you could have met him, but Barbara knew him."

I took the phone back from Sam to ask Micheline if she had been to any Delaunay shows back in the day.

"Why, of course," she said. And then Micheline launched into a story about how she and Paul had seen the groundbreaking Sonia Delaunay show at the Louvre Museum in 1964 and how much they had enjoyed it. She confided, "you know, I got curious and looked up Sonia Delaunay's obituary. At my age it's a very interesting section of the paper. She was born in 1885 and died in 1979 at 94 years of age. And to think that she was painting and exhibiting to the very end."

We chatted for a while about visiting soon to stay with her in Paris to see the latest exhibitions. I started to tell her about our visit to the glass workshop where they were mounting the window, but it was clear that Micheline wasn't really interested in those details. She announced that she had to hang up. Whew! She was a whirlwind.

I pushed the disconnect button on my phone. It immediately started ringing again and again with calls and messages from people who wanted to tell us how they had seen us on television. Eventually, even Melanie checked in from Florida. She had seen a little piece on our discovery on an internet news channel.

"Aunt Barbara," her strong voice boomed over the line. "Unbelievable! Of course, you had told me all about the tunnel and finding the glass for the window but now, television coverage! You're famous! And to think that I just missed all the excitement!"

"Yes, Melanie. But you were there at the meeting which started it all and helped to pin Thierry de Gonsalves down."

As the news spread out in an ever-widening circle from our close friends and family to distant acquaintances and half-forgotten connections, we basked in so much attention that we were happy when it started to die down. Which it did. Andy Warhol was correct. People had short attention spans. And in

France, although there was just as much interest in gossip as anywhere else, people also knew how to mind their own business and give others some space.

The village administration of Montpezat was finally thinking about us, however. They floated the idea that the names of those of us who had been instrumental in the discovery and installation of the Delaunay window should be inscribed on a plaque underneath it in the chapel.

In medieval times, the donors of stained-glass windows often had themselves portrayed kneeling in a bottom corner of the window they had sponsored. Laure, Pierre-Paul, the Bruneau's, Héloïse Dutroit, Sam and I all met to discuss the idea. We went back and forth, but in the end, we agreed to remain anonymous and let the window speak for itself.

As for the medieval tunnel, one of the most important finds of its kind in France since those in the town of Provins, up north, it would be studied in minute detail for many years, Especially the medieval graffiti which covered its walls. Until this research could be undertaken, the entry to the tunnel from Sam's and my house was definitively closed off. We could now return to live in our house as before. No wine cellar for Sam after all.

We were happy to move back into our higgledy piggledy little house after the grandeur of the Trois Terrasses. We expressed our gratitude to Daniel for his hospitality. It was nice to be on such good terms with him and leave the contretemps over the Judas tree behind.

As we slipped between the sheets covering the comfortable bed in our pretty bedroom overlooking the *collégiale* in the distance, Sam kissed me tenderly goodnight. I kissed him back and we lay there spooning feeling content and pleasantly drowsy.

Life was a continuum. People and events were always changing. Best to appreciate this delicious feeling while it lasted, I thought to myself.

"Penny for your thoughts," Sam said, nuzzling the back of my neck. *Had he sensed my mood?* Maybe it was only natural to feel a bit melancholy as the excitement surrounding our discoveries wound down.

"Oh, Sam!" I said melodramatically. "Don't ever change! Let's not ever change!"

"No problem," he reassured me. "*Pas de problème.* You have my word. *Je te jure.*"

"Why, Sam, your French is really improving," I complimented him.

"Thank you, Barbara, I have a good teacher. Very strict though."

We both laughed at that. Then yawning, we turned over to our respective sides of the bed and fell asleep.

Life returned to normal. Soon it would be time to pack up for our annual return to Sarasota. As usual, I was procrastinating about getting organized when the postman, *le facteur,* slid a letter under our front door. We didn't receive much snail mail. and it got my attention right away as it was a very official looking envelope with elegant lettering on triple bond paper stock. When I ripped open the heavy envelope, the letter it contained was headed by an impressive, embossed seal.

I read that Laure Acosta-Moneda, Pierre-Paul Achambault, Claude Bruneau, Sam and I would all be decorated with the prestigious *légion d'honneur* for our contribution to preserving the cultural patrimony of France. I could hardly contain my excitement. I ran upstairs and showed Sam, and we ran over to Laure's to see if she had got the news, which she had. We were all as delighted as could be. "La légion d'honneur," Pierre-Paul intoned reverently. "It's a dream come true. I can't stop pinching myself."

"But, what shall we wear?" I asked Laure. "I think some serious clothes shopping is called for here."

And that was how six months later, on a gloriously sunny winter day, we stood together at the Élysée Palace in Paris as the President of France kissed our cheeks and pinned the little *bleu, blanc et rouge rosette* on our dresses and jacket lapels. We glowed with pride and pleasure as he thanked us. Through our efforts, the Sonia Delaunay window had been rescued from oblivion. In his short speech, he quoted Françoise Giroud, French Minister of State for Women's Affairs, who said, "Sonia Delaunay was a dazzling creative force, rediscovered and found to be in vibrant harmony with our times." He continued, "Françoise Giroud was writing in 1975, but the same could easily be said today. As the *New York Times* wrote about her when she died in 1979, *Sonia Delaunay was a painter of exceptional gifts, an artist whose versatility was almost without parallel, and a source of ideas that never went out of style.*"

Speaking of style, the president's wife was there, too, a vision of classic French elegance in her Louis Vuitton suit. Her skirt was so short, and her heels were so high, we marveled at her ease climbing to the landing at the top of the palace steps, *le perron*, where the pinning-on ceremony took place.

Melanie was there for the grand occasion along with her mother, Amanda, and all my family and Sam's family, too. Each of us honorees was accompanied by a big group of relatives and friends. No one wanted to miss this once in a lifetime opportunity to be at the Élysée Palace and watch their loved one receive France's highest civil honor.

During the legion d'honneur ceremony, the President singled out an older gentleman in the audience who he introduced as Sonia Delaunay's grandson, Jean-Louis Delaunay. The Delaunays had had a son, Charles, who died in 1988, and this man was Charles' surviving child.

After the ceremony, we *mousquetaires* had an opportunity to talk with him. It was gratifying how grateful he was for our efforts to bring a lost one of his grandmother's works to light.

The whole day was a sublime experience followed by a delicious late lunch at an excellent restaurant in Laure's Paris neighborhood. Our party was so numerous that we took over the whole establishment and we lingered so long talking and laughing with each other that the management finally asked us to leave so they could prepare for the dinner hour.

EPILOGUE

It was two years before the Sonia Delaunay window was ready to be revealed to the public. Our same little group were among the honored guests and dignitaries at the *collégiale* for the grand unveiling. Sadly, Monsieur Bruneau, Frédéric's father, was absent, having passed away. He was represented by his son.

We had the pleasure of being among the first to view the newly installed Sonia Delaunay window. It was exquisite! Although boldly abstract in style, it somehow harmonized with and enhanced the famous medieval tapestries. They seemed to be having a dialogue with one another across the centuries as the play of sunlight streamed through the stained-glass window of the side chapel onto a pillar of the nave and illuminated the tapestry panels behind the altar.

Of course, many people did not like the new window. They thought it was too modern. They wanted to know what it was exactly. They couldn't make heads or tails of its abstract forms and geometric shapes. "It's scandalous, a travesty, outlandish," the naysayers said.

However, like the Eiffel Tower in Paris, which was execrated and ridiculed when it was erected in 1900, as time went by, it grew on the populace. First it was accepted and after a time, it became a beloved icon, a symbol of the city, a symbol of France.

So, it went with the Sonia Delaunay window. As the years passed, the *Montpezatais* became accustomed to the interesting, daring window in their church. They appreciated the excitement it generated among the tourists and the art lovers it attracted to the village. After a while, they couldn't remember a time when the modern stained-glass window hadn't been there. The collégiale would have seemed empty without it. It became a point of village pride.

From the start, the Delaunay window proved to be a huge attraction in the *Tarn-et-Garonne* and beyond, and it drew many visitors to Montpezat. So much so that Sam and I decided to move farther up the *rue de la Libération* where the tourist activity was less concentrated.

Our new house also dated from the 15th century, Montpezat de Quercy's heyday. It was located near the school and the *médiathèque* that was housed in the 17th century convent of *les Ursulines,* which boasted a beautiful cloister.

"Wouldn't it be something if there turned out to be a mystery associated with *les Ursulines* and the nunnery?" I said to Sam one day.

Sam raised his glass of *Côteaux du Quercy* wine and replied, "it surely would, *ma chérie.* It surely would. I'm always up for another adventure."

LA FIN?

AUTHOR'S NOTE

This book is a combination of fact and fiction. Sonia Delaunay was an actual person, and her life story and accomplishments are real. The Collégiale Saint Martin and its tapestries in Montpezat de Quercy, France also really exist, although there are actually fifteen tapestries in all. They have recently undergone a painstaking and expert restoration and are shown off to great advantage in their original setting in the apse of the church. It costs two euros to see them. The money activates a mechanism which opens their protective curtain and turns on a light to illuminate them for fifteen minutes.

Although there really is documentation that Mme Delaunay was commissioned in 1966 to decorate a church in Montpezat de Quercy, there is no such modern artwork to be found there.

DISCUSSION GROUP QUESTIONS

- Did the center of the art world shift after WWII? Where to? Why?
- What is a *viager* agreement? Do we have the same thing in the United States?
- In real life, the 1966 Sonia Delaunay stained-glass window project in Montpezat de Quercy never came to pass. Why not? Do you have any thoughts about that? Could it have anything to do with Sonia herself?
- Do you think modern artwork installed in medieval churches or historical buildings adds or detracts from the setting? Can you cite any examples from your experience?
- What do you think of the Cathedral of Notre Dame de Paris, recently re-built after the destructive fire?

ACKNOWLEDGMENTS

I would like to thank my writing coach, Lisa Pulitzer, for her encouragement and support and expertise. The members of our writing group at Long Island University helped to keep me moving along on this project. My editor, Gill McKnight, helped fine tune the manuscript. I am also grateful to my first readers, my neighbor and friend, Nadine Helstroffer and Susan King, my Florida friend and travel companion (China and French Polynesia).

I relied on Axel Madsen's excellent biography, *Sonia Delaunay, Artist of the Lost Generation* for source material about the artist's life. A visit to the 2024 "Sonia Delaunay" exhibition at the Bard Center for Decorative Arts in New York City was also instructive. It presented the opportunity to see some of Sonia's works, clothes, designs, notebooks, photos, films, illustrations and other ephemera, in person. Heartfelt thanks are also due to all my friends and acquaintances in the village of Montpezat de Quercy, France. The wonderful times I have spent there were a big part of my inspiration for this book.

Most of all, I want to recognize the contribution of my partner, Nathan Kujawski. His patience and encouragement throughout the project made its completion possible.

ABOUT THE AUTHOR

Roberta Samuels earned degrees in French and Art History from Northwestern University and the University of Paris at the Sorbonne. Her Art Mystery Novella series evolved from her passion for French culture, beautiful objets d' art, and exotic travel. The starting point for the books is based on her experience living in a medieval house in a French village interwoven with historical background and actual events and people. She worked as a French teacher, translator, tour escort and art gallery owner, showing her own artwork among others. She speaks French fluently. She lives in New York City and Montpezat de Quercy, France, with her partner.

Robertasamuels.com

 instagram.com/Rosamu1_